Anthony

By Teddy Milne

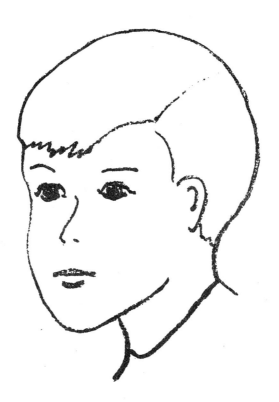

Anthony, by Teddy Milne
with illustrations by Teddy Milne

Copyright © 1986 by Teddy Milne
All rights reserved.
Library of Congress Catalog Card No. 86-062446
ISBN 0-938875-01-9

First Printing 1986   Printed in U.S.A.
10 9 8 7 6 5 4 3 2 1

Published by
PITTENBRUACH PRESS, 15 Walnut St., PO Box 553,
                    Northampton, MA 01060 USA

To order this book, send price as marked, plus $1.50
postage and handling, to PITTENBRUACH PRESS at the
above address.

Other books by the same author:
  "Choose Love." A vision of some changes we could
      make in ourselves and our culture in order
      to ensure global survival and a brighter
      future. Pittenbruach Press 1986.
  "War is a Dinosaur, and other songs of hope, love
      and weltschmerz." Includes a section on how
      to play piano or guitar "by ear." Also the
      haunting song, "Greenham Common's Gone."
      Pittenbruach Press 1987.
  "Peace Porridge Hot." Reasons for hope in the
      future -- peace WILL overcome. A collection
      of articles and useful information from the
      children's peace newsletter LASER. For age
      9 to 90. Pittenbruach Press 1987.

C H A P T E R   1
****

For once, the Home was quiet. You could even hear Big Ben striking the hour, way across the river. Anthony lay on his bunk, hands behind his head, listening to the distant bongs, and dreaming.

He was in a family, of course -- that was always the basis of his day-dreams -- and as usual it was a wealthy, titled family. His mother, the duchess, swept in on her way to a garden party at the palace, smelling delicious and wearing a feathery dress that tickled when she bent over to kiss him.

Anthony, his eyes closed, smiled. So did she. "Be good now, and I'll bring you home some cakes from the Queen's own kitchen." She smoothed his hair and kissed his cheek.

"Give Her Majesty my love."

Her laughter was like music. She moved toward the door, blowing him another kiss.

"Don't, don't!" A scream of terror broke into the dream and brought Anthony back to reality with a start.

He was on his feet almost before he realized it, and then hesitated. Giles, that new little kid, was kicking and pummeling Ronnie, the Home's resident bully, while Ronnie held something out of Giles' reach with one hand and pushed at the smaller boy's chest with the other. Ronnie was laughing, with that crow-like laugh he had.

"What's that you've got, Ronnie?" Anthony called out carefully and lightly.

"Looks like some kind of picture. Film star, I think." Ronnie laughed again as Giles, sobbing, tried to kick him again.

"Give it back! It's my mother! Give it back!" Giles sounded really terrified that he was going to lose the picture, and Anthony fought down a feeling of sympathy. That was not the way to handle Ronnie.

"Let me see it, can I?" He walked casually over to the two struggling boys and took the picture from Ronnie's hand. Giles gasped and bit his lip, panting with despair and fury.

"Hm. Looks just like you, Giles. Nice face." Anthony held it for Ronnie to see. "Same curly blonde hair, same baby blue eyes, same round face -- no mistake, it's your mother all right." He studied it for his own pleasure, swallowing the lump in his throat. A picture of someone's mother, even if she had died recently and abandoned Giles to the tender mercies of Washburn Home for Boys, was worth looking at. SHE looked as if she cared, all right. Not like the staff at the Home.

Looking at the picture, Anthony could feel a welling up of all his longings for being a member of a family, a real family, instead of one of 15 boys whom nobody really cared about.

Ronnie grabbed the picture back, and Anthony didn't try to stop him. "Pretty nice, huh?" He bent his head next to Ronnie's as they both looked at it again. Giles, pale and frozen, stood staring at them.

Anthony sighed. "But right's right, Ronnie, you can't take the kid's picture of his mother. That's like stealing a Bible."

Rather to his surprise, Ronnie grunted and threw the picture on the bed. Giles leaped on it, rolled across the bed in one quick move and sped out of the room.

Anthony and Ronnie eyed each other with no expression on their faces. Ronnie hadn't bothered with Anthony -- yet -- because Anthony had never had anything Ronnie wanted. And he normally kept out of Ronnie's way. But he knew there would probably come a time when Ronnie would turn on him. Ronnie liked to have everyone under his thumb.

Or perhaps it's just that people get into habits, Anthony thought to himself. He hasn't gotten into the habit of fighting with me, so he never thinks of it. Hope it stays that way.

"Wish I had a picture of MY mother." Anthony smiled lazily. "I'm not even sure I had one."

Ronnie laughed, and turned away.

Anthony sauntered from the room, feeling the

tension leave him as soon as he was out the door of the dormitory. Whew!

The encounter had bothered him, even though it had ended all right. Feeling restless, Anthony went on down the wide, old-fashioned staircase, feeling the dark, smooth banister under his hand, his eyes shifting away from the unvarnished section in the middle of every step, where a carpet was supposed to be.

Giles was cowering at the foot of the stairs, waiting for him.

"Will you be my friend?" he whispered, wasting no time.

Anthony sighed. "And protect you from Ronnie, you mean? Not on your nellie! I've got enough troubles."

Giles' face fell, and Anthony softened.

"Don't worry about Ronnie. Just keep out of his way, and with any luck he'll be sent to Borstal before he notices you again."

"What's a Borstal?"

"Oh, you know, where they send the really bad ones."

Giles' eyes grew large. "Is it worse than here, then?"

Anthony laughed. "Much worse! You don't know how lucky you are."

"I'm a good boy, my m-mother always s-said..."

Anthony sighed as Giles started blubbering again. Should he bother telling him that crying would only get him into trouble? No, what was the use? He'd find out soon enough.

Anthony crossed the darkly panelled hallway to the big front door with the stained glass window in it.

Pulling it open, he went out to sit on the front steps, watching the traffic go by and picking out the cars he would like to buy when he was rich.

The sexton was raking leaves on the tiny lawn of the church next door, and they waved to each other.

"I couldn't believe what I just heard," a voice behind him said, as the big door banged shut. Anthony turned as Gerry came out and sat beside him. "You took on Ronnie, and don't even have any bruises to show for it?" Gerry mockingly started examining his arm.

Anthony stifled a laugh. "Don't say anything, for goodness' sake. If he hears you, he'll be sure to fix that." He sighed and shook his head. "What I wouldn't give to get away from here."

"Not again! I thought you'd given up after last time."

"Oh, I get discouraged for a while, but then I look around and start dreaming of a family again, and my feet begin to itch."

It was Gerry's turn to shake his head. "But you must have tried everyone already!"

"No, I only got up to the 'O's. I think I'll take up where I left off."

Anthony had spent two years already on his re-search -- looking through Burke's Peerage until he found some young man who had died about the time Anthony was born, and then going to the library to dig up photographs, to see if there might be a family resemblance that would be useful.

"It's finding the pictures of the family that's the hard part," he muttered, half to himself.

"But what about Giles' mother?"

"What about her?" Anthony turned a puzzled face to meet Gerry's gaze.

"Well, Giles looks like his MOTHER, not his father, so why do you even need to have a family resemblance?"

Anthony's face broke into a wide grin as the idea took hold. "That's right -- super! I'm going to start right now! And after I get to the end of the book, I can start over again to pick up the ones I might have missed." He was on his feet.

Gerry snorted. "You're crazy! When are you going to get realistic? We're too old to get adopted. Might as well adjust and make the best of it. I plan to. I'll do well in school, get a good job, and then get married and start a family of my own. That's the only thing to do."

"But that would take years and years! Not me. I'm still small for my age, but once I sprout up, as you did this summer, it'll be too late. I just have to get out of here, Gerry. I really can't stand it. There's just this big -- ache in my chest all the time. Every night I dream about being in a family, where..."

"Where people care about each other. I know, you've said it before, a FEW times. But aside from

Ronnie, what's so bad about here? Aren't you and me friends, for instance?"

"Sure we are, Gerry. But, well, I just have to try, that's all."

"You're a dreamer."

Anthony shrugged. "So, I'm a dreamer. What's so terrible about that?"

"Nothing, nothing! Go ahead and dream. I'm just sorry for you, that's all." There was an unaccustomed scowl on Gerry's freckled face.

"You don't get anywhere by not trying." Anthony's voice was getting sulky.

"I hope you're going to wait until spring, at least. It's nearly November. Not a good time to go sleeping in doorways."

Anthony looked at him in dismay. Wait until spring! Now that he had this new idea, there seemed no time to waste. Anyway, perhaps -- perhaps the colder it was, the more sympathy people might have for him. He could feel himself blush, ashamed to say what he was thinking.

"I'd better get started," he said, turning to go inside.

"Anthony?"

"What?"

"What if they don't let you come back, next time? They might send you to a Borstal."

"Why would they?"

"It'll be the third time -- you haven't forgotten Stanley, have you?"

Anthony shivered. Stanley hadn't been all that bad, but he kept running away, and he'd been sent to Borstal last year. Nobody had ever heard from him again. "I've got to chance it, while I still can," he said stubbornly.

Gerry shook his head slowly. "I wouldn't want to live in a place that was full of Ronnies -- full of worse-than-Ronnies."

"Then wish me luck."

Gerry grunted. "I give up. Good luck, then."

The library on the second floor was Anthony's favorite room. It had a pleasant bow window with golden stained glass around the edges, so that it always looked as if the sun were shining in. The window overlooked the church garden next door, and you could almost think you were in the country, what with the smell of roses and cut grass that drifted up.

But there was work to do. Anthony turned away and looked over at the book he wanted.

Burke's Peerage was on the bottom shelf. Anthony could sit on the floor, with his back against the shelf, and read without being noticed. Anthony closed his eyes, wishing with all his might that the book would somehow find him a family to live in. Then he opened the book at "P" and settled down to read.

Packard. Hm, no. Paisley...

An hour later, he had nearly given up for the day. The print was so fine and the details so boring, he had almost fallen asleep, and the shelf was biting into his back. But he shook himself, changed position, and went on.

He had read into the next family before he realized what he had just read. His own name! Anthony Richard Martin, right there! And -- he could feel the hair on the back of his neck start tingling, and his hands felt clammy -- not only that, the other Anthony had died in a motor accident just six months before he was born!

Anthony started to shake, and had to put the book down. His heart was banging painfully against his chest. Had he dreamed it? Was it actually possible -- but he had lost the page, and scrabbled through the book to find it again.

Rothwick. He had been, this other Anthony, the Earl of Rothwick's son. The earl had died four months after his son's accident, and the title had gone to the younger son, Roger. Hmm. The new earl had been married to Lady Daphne Young. Three daughters. Castle Rothwick, Yorkshire.

Anthony got down the atlas and pored over the maps of Yorkshire, finally locating a tiny pinpoint that said "Castle Rothwick." His heart was thumping so loudly, it seemed to echo in the still room. This wasn't make-believe, this was real. He stared at the map, starting to picture the castle rising from a high cliff, flags flying from the turrets.

He had to go there, he had to!

But how would he get there? That was the main thing. He bent over the maps again, tracing the roads with his finger. There was a road from York to Scarborough, then a side road -- he whispered the route number with eyes closed, to make sure he'd remember.

Thoughtfully, he put the atlas back on the shelf. Yorkshire. In the back of his mind hung a question: could I really be the son of that Anthony? The present earl's nephew? He didn't dare think about it. It was too tempting, and would hurt too much if he failed. No. He was his own self. His real parentage didn't matter. All he wanted was some way to get into the family -- even a family with three girls!

Anthony looked out the golden windows at the setting sun. How on earth would he get all the way up to Yorkshire? And it was already getting cold, Gerry was right about that. He looked down at his green pullover, a left-over from when he'd been in the cub scouts. It was warm, but -- the winter coats were put away and wouldn't be brought out again until goodness knew when. A pullover wasn't much use if you were caught out in the cold at night. Should he go, quickly, before it got any colder, or wait until he got a coat, perhaps too late to go anywhere?

Daylight was another thing to consider. The sun was already setting at tea time -- by next month there wouldn't be much daylight to travel in.

He looked down at Burke's again, caressing the gold letters and trying to decide. This was Friday. Saturday would be the best day to go, when there was no school and he wouldn't be so noticeable. But that didn't leave him much time to think.

He sighed, and put the book back on the shelf.

There was an old-fashioned mirror over the desk, and he wandered over to look at his reflection. If his mother had a face like his, what would she look like? Intense brown eyes, hair the color of conkers, thin face -- maybe she wouldn't look so sad when she smiled. He smiled, picturing her for the first time. I don't need a photograph, he thought.

Wonder what the Rothwicks look like?

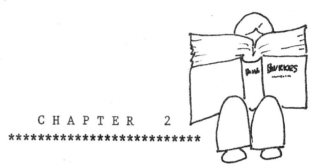

C H A P T E R   2
****

The bell gonged out in the hall, and Anthony heard thumps and bangs as the other boys leaped for the stairs.

Anthony scowled. I don't really like crowds of people, he thought, regretfully. Just a nice quiet family, orderly, serene. Nobody yelling and punching.

And a mother, of course. Not hired help that were always too busy and flustered, strict and businesslike and never a kiss or a hug. You'd think in a church home like this there'd be a little more affection, he thought, wondering again if kids in other Homes, with different staff, might be getting a better deal.

Anthony sighed. Probably not -- wouldn't all the grownups be just as busy?

He slid "Burke's Peerage" back onto the shelf, realized he was hungry, and ran down the stairs to the gloomy dining room with its dark panelling and darker wallpaper. Not my favorite room, he thought.

Everyone else was already at the table, and he had to take a seat beside Ronnie. Miss Rice said grace and they sat down. Ronnie kicked him under the table on one side and Ken kicked him on the other.

"You kept us waiting thirty seconds," Ken hissed.

"Forty-five," prompted Steve from across the table.

"Boys," Miss Rice said. Annie sped around the table with plates of food. At least the food was good, Anthony thought, his eyes lighting up as Annie put a plate of chicken and chips in front of him. I suppose at Rothwick Castle they have a French chef. Maybe they eat snails and things!

"Carl's got a job in the chip shop on Ferry Street," Fred announced, and everyone cheered.

Carl blushed. "Well, I turned 16 two weeks ago. 'Bout time I started earning my way." He gave Fred a friendly poke. "Maybe I can get you a job there come March."

"Never mind a job, just nick us some chips," Ronnie said with a harsh laugh.

Ralph, who was 17 and worked in a car repair shop in East London, punched Ronnie in the arm. Ralph was the only one big enough to get away with it -- though no one knew for sure whether he was really as tough as he looked. He hardly ever said anything except "Pass the salt."

Anthony looked around the table. They were supposed to sit in order of age, with the little ones down near Miss Rice and Annie, but the older boys usually tried to avoid sitting next to Ronnie and Miss Rice had given up trying to keep them in order. Anyway, she had her hands full, helping two-year old

Charlie and three-year-old Jacky. Annie sat between Larry, who was four, and Dick, who was six. Giles came next, picking at his food. Tommy was teasing him again, trying to take his chicken.

Next came Ned and Steve, who were almost Anthony's age, but they did everything together and hardly talked to anyone else. Maybe they stuck together to keep Ronnie away. Ken was 13 like Ronnie, only a year older than Anthony and Gerry, but he liked to read all the time and had his hands full keeping Ronnie from picking fights.

The only one Anthony could really call a friend was Gerry -- and Gerry was so stick-in-the-mud! Anthony sighed. And he was giving him the silent treatment tonight. No, somehow they just plain didn't come together as if they were a family. Maybe if the older ones helped -- if Ralph wasn't so quiet, or Carl didn't stay away all the time, they could have helped keep things under control. Fred was next in line, but he was hopeless. Fell over his own feet, ate too much, just let himself be a punching bag.

And after Fred came Ronnie. But even before Ronnie had come, three months ago, all the boys had fought and teased and shoved all day long, and Anthony was tired of it.

Hey, I've been testing to see if I really want to leave here, Anthony realized as Annie set a dish of steaming apple crumble in front of him. And yes, I really do.

I'll never get another chance like this one -- my own name and all -- how can I just wait around until spring, like Gerry says I should? If he thought he had a relative, wouldn't he be off like a shot? Sure he would. And it's getting colder every day. I can't wait another week -- can I?

"Boys!" Miss Rice called out, and Anthony realized Ken and Fred were wrestling noisily, their dessert finished.

"You may be excused!" She shook her head in despair at them, but she herself still had a way to go before Charlie was fed -- he was making mashed potatoes out of his chips, and didn't seem to like the cut-up bits of chicken, either.

The boys dashed for the door, pushing and shoving, and most of them went on out to the back courtyard, where a rough and tumble game of soccer was the usual after-dinner sport.

"Coming, Anthony?" Gerry was waving to him. Anthony shook his head and watched as the boys pushed and yelled their way out the door.

Anthony started slowly up the stairs. I have to think this thing through, he told himself -- but how can I? I don't know anything about these Rothwicks. What if it turns out to be like the other two times? He sighed again. But he couldn't just pay no attention to that magic coincidence in "Burke's."

He went on up to the library again, hoping for some time alone to think.

It was Saturday morning, and Anthony sat on the polished brown stairs, his stomach in a knot, still trying to decide what to do. He could hear the older boys quarreling upstairs, and the younger ones quarreling downstairs. Giles was sniffling somewhere nearby.

What a cry-baby, he thought, and then was immediately ashamed. After all, until recently Giles had lived in a real home; coming to this dump after that must be even worse than growing up here.

Some joke, calling this a Home, Anthony thought moodily, running his hand idly up and down one of the smooth stair spindles. There was no family feeling here, no one to really care about you -- Anthony's mind switched off at that thought. It didn't do to think that way. He turned instead to one of his favorite daydreams, that he was the young Edward in "Prince and the Pauper," unrecognized and despised, but a true prince underneath. Or sometimes the other way around, playing the pauper dressed up as the prince -- the nice thing about daydreams was you could play both parts.

Annie swept by, down in the front hall, putting the big porridge bowl away. It was a wonder it was still in one piece -- it had been Fred's turn to help in the kitchen, and Fred was hard on china.

Tommy ran into the hall, followed by a yowling Dicky, followed by Miss Rice, her face red from running.

"Give that back!" resounded from upstairs. The house was in full swing. Anthony closed his eyes, tuning it all out. His thoughts drifted away.

They were parading through the streets of London, on the way to Westminster Abbey to crown Anthony King of England. Anthony shifted uncomfortably beneath the weight of his heavy royal robes, as the people cheered and tossed their caps into the air.

Anthony bowed solemnly. He had promised the chancellor that he would go through the ceremony without protest, for the good of England, but inside he felt like one of Annie's puddings. What would happen when the real prince -- or rather, the real king -- turned up?

"Anthony!" A voice rang faintly in the noise of the crowd, but Anthony heard it, and turned. His mother! There she was, her sweet face staring at him in astonishment. Yes, SHE would know him, no matter how he was disguised. She pushed towards him in the crowd, and he reached toward her. Then he remembered, and pulled his hand back. He glanced fearfully toward the chancellor, who towered beside him.

His mother struggled through the line of soldiers, almost touching Anthony's polished boot.

"Seize that woman!" The chancellor's voice boomed out, and Anthony, horrified, watched as two soldiers grabbed his mother roughly.

"Stop!" Astonished, Anthony realized it was he who had shouted. He swallowed hard, trying desperately to think. Then he sat straighter on his stallion. After all, was he not king?

"Let this be a happy day," he said grandly, imitating the chancellor, at whom he didn't dare look. "The woman's only crime is that she loves her king. Bring a horse and let her ride in the procession. I shall speak with her later."

The chancellor was looking at him strangely, but with respect, and said nothing. His mother looked confused. The crowd cheered.

"On to Westminster!" Anthony waved to the happy crowd, and the procession, which now included his mother clinging desperately to the mane of a horse, started in motion again. I shall give my mother a place at court, Anthony was thinking. Why had I not thought of that before? He felt a warm glow in his heart.

The ringing of a doorbell interrupted his dream and caused a sudden stillness in the house. Everything seemed suspended for a moment, even the smallest boys turning away from their battles in surprise.

Visitors!

Miss Rice reappeared, gave her mousey brown hair a quick pat by the hall mirror, and opened the door.

"Oh, Mrs. Woods, how kind of you to come and see us! Do come in." She opened the door wide as two large women came in, folding their umbrellas. A chauffeur in a uniform put a large carton inside the door and left again.

Anthony tensed as Mrs. Woods murmured introductions and the three women moved into the sitting room. He knew what was coming next: rounding up the "poor dears" while Mrs. Woods talked about how shabby they looked, as if they weren't really there. Then she'd hand out her sons' outgrown clothes, expecting everyone to be hysterical with gratitude.

That was one problem with the Home having ancient ties with the church next door -- the parishioners thought they had a right to visit and pry and act superior.

Making a sudden decision, Anthony got to his feet, slid down the last few feet of banister, and ducked into the closet under the stairs, burrowing his way into the back.

He was just in time. He could hear Miss Rice calling them, all 15 of them by name, to come and see what "lovely Mrs. Woods" had brought.

The closet had a smell of old rubber boots in it, a pretty powerful pong, but Anthony tried breathing through his mouth, and that helped some. He could hear murmurings through the wall, and shook his head sorrowfully. He knew what the boys were thinking, every last one of them -- that maybe this new lady would be looking for someone to adopt. Why did it seem as if he alone recognized that all the standard orphan dreams of Parents Discovered, Parents Earned, Parents Won, Parents Bestowed by Fairy Godmothers, were all fated to remain empty dreams? In his twelve years at the Home there had never been a successful adoption that he knew of -- maybe the adoption agencies had forgotten about Washburn. In any case, the dreams persisted, and the boys all seemed content to stay at the Home and wait for their lucky day.

Well, thought Anthony savagely, hugging his knees, HE wasn't waiting for that way out any more. He was doing his own looking, thank you. These Rothwicks, now. They took a bit of thinking about. Lady Daphne. What a beautiful name that was! The affectionate Duchess of yesterday's dream suddenly became the Lady Daphne, presiding over a ball at Rothwick Castle.

"And this is our son, Anthony," she was saying to the assembled throng. A lusty cheer filled the glittering hall, setting the crystal chandeliers tinkling.

The three daughters hovered in the shadows, beaming adoringly at him.

It was a costume ball, and he was dressed as Prince Edward, son of Henry the Eighth (but was he really the prince, or the pauper?)

Anthony lay back in the dark closet, smiling.

"My dear, aren't they just pathetic?" suddenly boomed through the wall from the next room. Anthony opened his eyes and then shut them again, tight. "Wouldn't one just love to take them all home with one?"

Anthony winced angrily. How unfair of Mrs. Woods to get their hopes up that way! He folded his arms around his head to block his ears. His stomach felt tight, and he tried to take a deep breath to relax, nearly choking on the smell of the closet.

Those awful women! Would they never go away? Why did Miss Rice let them talk that way? He gritted his teeth as he pictured Miss Rice looking sternly at him, hands on hips. He stuck his tongue out, and then wriggled, trying to get more comfortable. He willed himself back into his dream.

"Now, Anthony, you really must dance with the Princess. She's expecting it." Lady Daphne smiled at him indulgently, and kissed his forehead.

"All right, Mother."

"Oh, my diamond necklace -- it's gone!" Lady Daphne turned pale, clutching at her bare neck.

"Don't worry, mother, I'll find it. You must have dropped it somewhere." Anthony turned, and caught a glimpse of a sinister-looking man sidling out of the ballroom through one of the French windows.

"Stop!" Anthony sped after him into the dark garden, felling him with a Rugby tackle.

The guests were pouring out of the ballroom to watch. "Bravo, Anthony!" they shouted, as he took the glittering diamond necklace from the man's pocket and held it up for everyone to see.

The crowd moved respectfully out of his way as he strode manfully toward the castle terrace where his mother waited, a look of adoration and admiration in her eyes. "My dearest boy,'" she murmured as he approached.

"For he's a jolly good fellow," the crowd began to sing...

The sudden rush of feet on the stairs above his head woke Anthony. He could hear muffled goodbyes, and as the front door closed, he started to breathe a sigh of relief -- but cut it short when the pong reached him again.

He pawed his way to the closet door and slipped out into the hall. He was heading for the front door for some fresh air when Miss Rice appeared in front of him.

For once, she didn't seem disapproving. "Oh, Anthony, there you are. You missed some lovely visitors. I saved this school blazer for you -- it's really quite nice this time -- it's hardly been worn. I'm sure it's your size -- do try it on."

She held it for him, and Anthony slid his arms into the sleeves. "You're right on both counts, Miss Rice -- it fits, and it's super!" Anthony couldn't keep the surprise out of his voice. He felt a bit contrite, too, after what he'd just been thinking of her. She wasn't such a bad sort, and 15 boys is a lot to handle. I'm an ungrateful brat, he thought.

The navy blue jacket was soft and warm, and made him feel like an ordinary boy for once, instead of an object of charity. It even made his handed-down cub-scout pullover look good.

He turned, and met Ronnie's jealous stare. Ronnie nodded slightly, his face expressionless but his pale eyes challenging him.

Anthony felt a chill, in spite of the warm blazer. They all knew what Ronnie's stares meant. You had to know, to survive. He was picking Anthony as the next victim for a fight. It wasn't enough that Anthony had interfered between Ronnie and Giles, now he'd gotten the best jacket. He saw Ronnie's eyes run down the jacket, saw Ronnie smile, and his heart sank.

"Help me with this box, will you, Ronnie?" Miss Rice said briskly.

Ronnie nodded to Anthony, as if to say "I'll get you later," and started dragging the box down the hall.

Anthony escaped out the door, taking a deep breath of the cold air. Even London air smelled good after that closet. He hugged the new jacket around him, feeling frustration welling up in him. What was the point of getting anything new, with Ronnie around?

He stood on the steps, his stomach tense, trying desperately to think. Did he dare to run away -- to try to get all the way to Yorkshire? He chewed his forefinger nervously.

Next door the church choir was practicing. A big red double-decker bus rumbled by up at the corner. Anthony sighed, remembering the other times he had tried to persuade a family to take him in -- disasters. Was he just being pig-headed? Maybe the Home wasn't all that bad. Maybe if he spent less time in the library, less time daydreaming by himself -- but there was that ache inside him that never went away.

He hesitated on the top step. Stay or go? Go or stay?

Suddenly the choir boomed out, "Be not afraid!"

Startled, Anthony looked across at the lighted windows. "Be not afraid!" came again.

Anthony straightened his back, feeling a tingling in his scalp. Almost without thinking, he ran lightly down the steps. He was doing it! An exultant smile lifted Anthony's face. Yes. He'd go, right now, before he had a chance to get scared, before Ronnie ruined his new jacket, before -- he faltered -- before lunch? Yes!

He forced himself to walk slowly down the quiet street. At the corner he looked back at the ugly brick building where he had spent most of his life.

He stared at it, thinking, "This time, no matter what, I won't go back."

Thinking, "But I say that every time."

Thinking, "Well, here goes. Once I cross Lambeth Bridge, it'll be too late."

Then he turned the corner and walked deliberately away.

C H A P T E R   3
****

The Rothwicks of Castle Rothwick were not in Yorkshire at the moment. They, too, were in London, only a few miles away from Washburn Home for Boys, at fashionable Melby Place, having a battle royal.

"None of you has the faintest idea what it's like to have work to do." The Earl of Rothwick spoke in an icy tone that was no less chilling although his family was used to it. His scar was a deep and prominent red, as it always got when he was angry. It made him look melodramatically sinister.

"But you promised, Daddy!" Elaine, the youngest daughter, said for the third time, her gray eyes stormy. "It's not fair, telling us at the last minute that we can't go til tomorrow, when we're all packed and ready. And you know how much we love it at Rothwick and how much we hate it here!"

"Hush, Elaine," her mother said sharply.

"Well, I hate it; and I don't care who knows it!"

"Daddy, couldn't you take us up and then come back earlier to finish your work?" Diana, the oldest daughter, was trying to be reasonable. "After all, it's the weekend." Her hand brushed her pale forehead as if she had a headache.

"Yes." The countess looked away at the wall. "What business can't wait on a weekend? Couldn't you take your papers with you?"

Rothwick winced. His wife always spoke as if he weren't there. That maddened him more than the children's contrariness. Unfortunately, he had no real answer for her logic. He hesitated.

"I don't see why we have to go at all." Beth, the middle daughter, flounced her blonde curls in that irritating way she had. "It's freezing up there this time of year, and anyway, I wanted to go riding." Her voice took on that wheedling tone that he detested. "Couldn't the rest of you go and let me stay here? You'd have more room in the car, anyway."

"We'll stay together." Rothwick spoke curtly. "And I've asked you to stop calling me 'Daddy.'" He suspected they did it just to prove to themselves he wasn't as dreadful as he looked, but still, it was a childish name for girls their age to be using.

"I don't know why we can't get a new car, we're too big for that old thing," Beth started, ignoring her father, but she was interrupted by the arrival of the girls' cousins.

"I say, we could hear you shouting from the library," Reggie sneered. "A spot of bother, eh?"

Elaine turned on him angrily. "I'll bother YOUR spots! This is none of your business."

"It is if you're disturbing our peace," put in Albert, belligerently. "But then, I realize it's frightfully difficult for you to control your family, Uncle Roger. They're a wilful lot, aren't they! One would think they had money!"

Everyone was struck silent by this bit of bad manners, and Rothwick made a swift decision. "All right, we leave in half an hour. But you realize it'll be late when we get there, and the house will be cold, and Sam hasn't been up there for two weeks -- you won't complain!" It was a command, rather than a question.

Elaine and Diane nodded, their faces brightening. Beth flounced her hair again, and pouted.

Rothwick scowled, wishing they wouldn't always force him to speak harshly. They never seemed to cooperate unless he got angry.

The three girls started out into the corridor. Elaine tripped over Bertie's thrust-out foot and swung on him angrily. Bertie danced out of reach, laughing, and Elaine chased him down the hall.

"If you ask me," Beth said saucily to Reggie, "it's Bertie that needs to be controlled."

"Boys will be boys," Reggie said loftily, as if he were not one himself.

"Well, well!" Rothwick's brother-in-law Frank appeared and clapped Rothwick on the shoulder. Rothwick gritted his teeth. "All taken care of?"

"I'm afraid we've decided to go up tonight after all." Rothwick moved out of Frank's reach.

Frank's puffy face took on a look of concern. "But, my dear boy, we need those figures tomorrow!"

"Surely they can wait until Monday? I'll take them up with me to work on..."

"That's not on, old boy. Can't let them leave the office -- suppose there were an accident?"

Rothwick turned pale, and so did Diana and Beth, who did an about-face in unison and walked away. When an accident had done so much damage to them all, it seemed impossibly unfeeling for anyone to say such as thing, even Frank, who was not noted for his tact.

"Now, now, don't take offense. Frankly, I think it's morbid the way all of you take on if anyone mentions accidents. Let's be realistic -- they happen all the time. And I can't take a chance on having those papers strewn all over the M-One."

"Then I'll come down again early Sunday and do it." Rothwick's tone was getting icier by the minute.

"Oh, there you are." Frank's wife, unbelievably the sister of Rothwick's quiet Daphne, came stalking down the hall. "Dinner will be early tonight, 7:30 sharp. Do try and get those girls of yours to be on time."

"My dear, Roger is trying to tell me they aren't staying after all."

"Nonsense. It's too late to drive up to Yorkshire now, it's nearly dark already." Victoria swept back her frosted blonde hair.

"There are lights on the car." Rothwick's sarcasm was lost on Victoria.

"But I've already ordered dinner for all of us. Daphne, do tell your husband you should stay."

Daphne turned her head slowly, reluctantly, to meet her sister's eyes. "What?" she said in that vacant way she had.

"You know perfectly well what I said," Victoria said in exasperation. "Marriage has certainly ruined you -- why don't you ever speak up for yourself?"

Daphne turned and looked out the window.

Rothwick felt his temper slipping out of control. "Plenty of time to tell the kitchen about the change, isn't there?" he growled.

Frank frowned. "I wanted Beth to meet young Lord Unger. He's coming around after dinner with his aunt. A very eligible young man."

"Good lord, Beth's only 14!"

"Nearly 15. Dear boy, the more young people she meets now, the better off she'll be when she starts going out to parties and such like."

Rothwick could feel his scar reddening again, and he turned and headed for the door, not bothering to answer.

Frank watched him go, still frowning. Then, with a shrug, he turned to his wife. "He's in one of his tempers tonight." His voice boomed down the hall. "Wouldn't you think he'd at least be civil, after all I've done for him?"

"Never mind, dear, come along. It will be nice having a weekend with just the family, for once."

All of them heard it, but everyone except Beth was too elated at the thought of getting away to worry about the suggestion that they were in the way at Melby Place.

Rothwick went to leave his briefcase in his office upstairs while the girls finished packing up the car.

When the Rothwicks were finally on the road in their ancient Morris, which was getting a bit cramped now that the girls were growing up, the wrangling started up again.

"Daddy, make Elaine stop!" Beth wailed from the back seat, pinching her sister.

"She's the one who's pinching," Elaine said angrily.

"Brat!"

"Witch!"

"Both of you, pack it in." Rothwick stole a glance at his wife, who was sitting impassively beside him, but as far away from him as she could get. Why was it always his job to stop the girls' quarrels?

As if he didn't know the answer to that. His wife paid no attention to them, whether they were quarreling or good as gold. Well, not that they were ever good as gold.

Diana was the only one who was no trouble. But that was because she was like her mother, always off in a world of her own. Perhaps it wasn't the best way for her to be growing up, but she seemed content enough. He glanced at her in the mirror. Her eyes were shut -- perhaps she was asleep. She wears her hair pulled back too severely, he thought, not for the first time.

Beth leaned forward and began chattering in his ear. "Uncle Frank says I'll be a champion shot one of these days," she said proudly. "And he's hinting that perhaps he'll buy me my own horse..."

"No. No horse."

"But Daddy, why? He said the stables look after private horses, and he said anyone with as good a seat as mine..."

Elaine hooted with laughter. "A good seat! Oh, that's rich!"

Beth put on her snooty look. "You ignorant girl," she said loftily. "You're just jealous because Uncle Frank doesn't take you riding."

"Anyway, you aren't getting a horse, Daddy just said so."

"If Uncle Frank is kind enough to give me a horse, I don't see how Daddy or anyone else can prevent it!" Beth was pouting now.

"There will be no horse." Rothwick's voice was very final.

Beth leaned back in the seat, her arms folded, and jabbed her elbow into Elaine, who kicked her in the ankle. Diana sighed.

The car moved on, the sunset unnoticed in the general misery. But there was one thought common to them all. At Rothwick there was room enough for all of them to get away from each other. Thank goodness for that!

C H A P T E R   4
****

Anthony's stomach was grumbling as loudly as the lorries on the bridge by the time he got as far as Westminster Palace. Out of habit, he had walked much of the way with his head down, searching the pavement for coins, but today he hadn't had any luck. Wouldn't you know, when he could have used some money for taking a bus out of the city. But perhaps he should be seeing the sights while he was about it.

He looked up at Big Ben, and gave it a smile. It was an old friend, at least to his ears. He paused and looked around him at the towering Houses of Parliament. A group of Japanese tourists were taking photos of each other, and an artist was sitting at an easel, painting.

Anthony wandered on, glancing timidly at the painting as he walked past. Then, getting curious, he sidled closer.

"I say, that's good!"

"You like it?" The artist glanced up briefly before returning to his work. He was painting the statue of Richard the Lion-Hearted. But it didn't look like a statue -- it looked alive.

"He looks real -- I mean, not as much of a hero as he's usually made out."

"Is he a hero to you?" The artist went on working as he talked.

"Not really. I mean, he abandoned England to go chasing after glory in the crusades, didn't he, and left the wrong people in charge."

"Sounds as if you've followed our Richard's career, at least."

"That's because my middle name is Richard. I suppose that made me interested."

"Mine is too -- how about that! But what about Richard the Second? Hero or not hero?" The artist squeezed some paint out of a crunched-up tube right onto the canvas, and squished it around with his brush. Anthony watched, fascinated, and then remembered the question.

"Richard the Second? He started off well, but he turned out badly, too, didn't he? He seemed so great when he met Wat Tyler and won everybody over. Why do you suppose he ended up as a failure?"

"Must be hard to be a king, especially at a young age. I wouldn't like to be one, would you?"

"There must be some nice things about it, I should think," Anthony mumbled, a bit embarrassed as he remembered his dreams.

The artist laughed. "What do you think of Richard the Third, then?"

"He's not anybody's hero."

"Oho, so you haven't read enough about him to know that isn't true! There's even a group known as 'Friends of Richard the Third.'"

"Are we talking about the same Richard? The one who murdered his nephews in the Tower?"

"The same. Only there seems to be some evidence that maybe he didn't do it."

"What evidence?"

"You'll have to look into it, yourself. I'm no historian. But I do know that Henry Tudor rewrote history so that people wouldn't start thinking they might have been better off under Richard."

Anthony's stomach gave an especially loud grumble just then, and the artist, without a pause in his work, said smoothly, "By the way, I wouldn't mind a sandwich. Look in that bag there, would you? I think there are several. Take one yourself."

"Th-thanks, I wouldn't mind." Anthony found the sandwiches and, after offering one to the artist, bit into another with great pleasure. Roast beef!

"I only share my lunch with fellow artists, actually. So you'd better try your hand at this, too." The artist held out a pad of paper and a pencil.

"Oh, I'm no good at drawing."

"Doesn't matter. There's something even more important, and that's being good at SEEING. Come on, have a go, and start seeing what you've missed so far."

Anthony took the paper and pencil, rather reluctantly, and made a tentative line or two. "Hm.

I see what you mean. I never would have noticed that muscle in the horse's leg..."

The artist took up another pad and started a quick sketch of Anthony. "What comes in front of Richard?"

"Oh, my name? It's Anthony."

The artist laughed. "Another coincidence. You've heard of Marc Anthony? Well, I'm the Marc part."

Anthony smiled at him. "But I wish you'd tell me more about Richard, Marc. If they've found out something different about him, why do all the history books still say he was the Wicked Uncle?"

"They couldn't change all the books, could they? And waste all that paper?" They both laughed.

"No one knows the whole story, but they've found out a few things, such as that Richard was the rightful king, not a usurper after all. So he didn't have to kill his nephews, they were not a threat to him. Turns out they were illegitimate, by the laws of the time, so they couldn't have inherited the throne anyway. It was Henry Tudor who needed to kill them off -- he destroyed the evidence that they were illegitimate, both to discredit Richard and also because he wanted to marry the boys' sister to strengthen his claim to the throne. But that made the boys rather awkward, you see? If their sister was legitimate, then so were they, which would mean..."

"That young Edward was king instead of Henry Tudor!"

"Right. But just what did happen to the nephews is still a mystery. Old Tudor did his work well, and poor Richard has been maligned all these years. From the evidence there is, he seems to have been a pretty decent king -- fair and just, generous -- all the virtues."

"Well, I'm glad to hear it -- glad there was one Richard, after all, who wasn't so bad."

"I trust you're going to be a staunch Yorkist from now on!"

"Yorkist?" Anthony felt a little thrill go up his backbone. "Yes -- yes, I am."

"Good. Too bad, isn't it -- the end of the Plantagenets. I always thought it was a pity."

"But I've never..."

"Never what?"

"Never understood why it was the end of them. It's just because we only use the father's name, isn't it. I mean, Henry the Eighth, and Elizabeth, too, weren't they pure Plantagenet in coloring, and personality, and everything? Henry's mother was a Plantagenet, and I've always thought they inherited everything from her. But they're known as Tudors, just because of the way names are set up."

Marc gave a pleased little laugh. "That's pretty good thinking -- it certainly never occurred to me, but I like the idea. Thanks, Anthony. It gives me an idea for another painting. How about this -- a family portrait of Henry VIII, Elizabeth -- and Edward IV and his daughter, Henry's mother -- showing the family resemblance?"

Anthony wriggled with pleasure.

Just then a horn beeped, over at the kerb, and a girl with long black hair and no make-up leaned out of a car and shouted, "Marc!"

Marc looked over at her blankly, and then smiled with delight.

"Jenny! Oh help, I forgot, didn't I!" He started packing up his things. "Sorry, Anthony, old boy. Forgot I was meeting her for lunch. Think she'll forgive me? Look, take the rest of the sandwiches, will you, so they won't go to waste? Oh, and here's a sketch of you, if you'd like it..."

"Of me! That's great -- thanks!"

"Good luck to you -- goodbye!" Marc strode off to meet the girl, trailing bits and pieces from his kit.

Anthony swallowed hard, feeling a momentary pang of regret. After all, though, did he expect every stranger to want to adopt him, just like those silly kids at the Home?

He looked down at the sketch in his hand, feeling pleased as well as forlorn. In the corner was scrawled, "To Anthony, from his friend Marcus Elliot."

Anthony folded it carefully in from the edges, so as not to have a crease across his face. He'd even, he decided, keep the sketch of Richard the Lion-Hearted he had begun, to remind him of their conversation.

Fancy getting to like old Richard the Third! Plenty of good story stuff there -- he could pretend to be the young nephew, Edward, escaping from Henry Tudor's men...

He turned toward Hyde Park, chewing thoughtfully on another sandwich as he went. No, he wouldn't turn back. Richard the Third wouldn't have turned back.

Richard the Third...

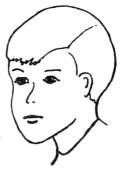

C H A P T E R   5
****

Anthony was hungry again by the time it started getting dark. His feet hurt, too. He walked on, waiting for it to be still darker before he found himself a place for the night. He was still in London, although he had worked his way well to the north of the city.

For a moment, the cold thought occurred to him that perhaps he was being stupid not to appreciate Washburn, which wasn't so bad -- it was rather like a big family, after all, with Miss Rice as the mother.

Funny, though, that nobody ever thought of her as their mother -- it was rather someone like Giles' picture, someone soft and loving, who would kiss you goodnight. Poor Miss Rice -- it must be hard to look after 15 boys; perhaps one couldn't really blame her for not being more motherly. Perhaps, even, no real mother could hope to measure up to his dreams. Anthony sighed.

Well, he had started, and he wasn't going to turn back this early in the game. That was it, look on it

as a game. If he won, great. If he lost, he'd be a
good sport, come what may.

Wait, here was an empty lot -- just the ticket.
He glanced up and down the street. Yes, it was dark
enough, and no one seemed to be about. He ducked
through a hole in the fence and looked around him in
the dim light. There was something over there -- it
looked like a packing crate. He stumbled over to it
and peered in. There seemed to be an old car seat or
something inside. What luck! He squeezed in and lay
down on it gratefully, thankful for the warm jacket.

He had barely closed his eyes when a light caught
him in the face and an aggrieved voice whispered,
"'Ere, wotcher doin' 'ere? This is our place. Out
you get!"

Anthony sat up, blinking in the light.

"Eh! You're just a kid! What you doin' 'ere?"
the voice repeated. This time Anthony recognized it
as a voice hardly older than his own.

"I've run away."

"Coo! You 'aven't!" There was a moment's
silence as this information was digested. "Well, all
right then, you can stay 'ere tonight. Just tonight,
mind!"

The light went off, and Anthony could see the boy
beckoning outside with his arm. Two more boys
appeared and the three squeezed into the crate,
squatting on the floor.

"Where you bound for?" The first boy looked at
Anthony curiously.

"Yorkshire." Anthony hugged his knees. It seemed so far away as to be impossible.

"Yorkshire! And you're walking?"

"I thought I could thumb a lift if I got far enough out of London."

"Mm," the boy said doubtfully.

"Wait a mo, Bob," said the second boy. "Remember we heard that bloke in your building say he was driving to Yorkshire tonight? I think it was Yorkshire."

"That's an idea! He's got a lorry he does odd jobs with."

"You think he'd take me?" Anthony asked eagerly.

All three boys laughed. "Not if he knew about it, not 'im." Bob rubbed his ear reflectively as if remembering a blow. "But if you could hide in the back, like, he wouldn't know about it until it was too late, would he!"

"'E wouldn't bring you back, anyways."

"Just be sure to get out of his way if he finds you."

Anthony grinned in the dark. "No problem."

"You live in Yorkshire?"

"Not yet, but I might," Anthony said, not untruthfully. As far as he knew. "I'm looking for relatives there." He glanced sideways at Bob. "I've run away from an orphan's home."

"Blimey!" The boys looked at him in admiration. This was even better.

"Had anything to eat? Here, Piggy, wot you got? You've always got something."

"Get your own, Bob, this lot's for me!" Piggy answered defensively from the darkness.

Bob laughed. "Me mum wouldn't really mind my nicking you some grub, but I'd have to watch out for me dad if he's home." He snorted derisively. "That is if by some miracle he's sober."

Anthony glanced at him curiously. He had never really imagined a father, he realized with some amazement. Fathers were cardboard figures. Mothers were real.

Piggy was being made to "fork over," and a bag of soggy crisps and a banana were thrust into Anthony's hands. He gulped them down, thinking about what Bob had said. Maybe family wasn't all it was made out to be in storybooks.

"What's it like, living in a family? I never have."

"Funny, I was just going to ask you what it's like living in one of them 'omes." Bob laughed. "Well, our family is just me and Mum and Da, and my dumb sister Agnes. And here's me cousin Donald, who lives across the street. I don't know, what's there to tell?"

Anthony shrugged. "I don't know -- just -- what do you do all day?"

"Oh, the usual day is I get up and light the fire and make me own breakfast and get off to school -- only two more years of that, thanks be. Then after school I muck about until supper time so I won't have to go home and do chores and listen to my sister going on about her hair and her clothes. I try to get there just late enough to eat what's left over, after the dishes are washed up, otherwise I might get roped into that. Then I go out again because by then the old man is likely to get steamed up over something and start smashing things. If I sneak home quietly after he's in bed it's all right. He gets up at five, you see, so he's away to bed before me. Then I go to bed and that's it. End of a perfick day."

Anthony looked at him in disappointment. How could it be that bad, he thought disconsolately.

"Come on," Bob said. "Your turn. Tell us about the orphan 'ome."

"It's nearly the same in one way, most of the day is school." They all exchanged glances of agreement on how school was. That was expected.

"We sleep in a big dormitory room, eight of us all lined up," Anthony went on.

"Coo, that must be fun,'" Donald said enviously. "Wish I had that many pals to be like brothers to me."

Anthony looked at him curiously, remembering that in fact it was fun, sometimes. "But some of the kids are so little," he protested, "and they cry all night, and you never have any privacy."

"Privacy! I sleep on the sofa in the sitting room. You think that's any privacy?" Piggy snorted.

"Well, anyway, we get up when the bell rings, and get dressed and go down to breakfast."

"A good cooked one, too, I'll bet. I'm ready to go -- tell me how to get there!"

Anthony laughed, and the boys laughed, too, but a little wistfully.

"Then you go to school? What do you do after?"

"We have to go straight back, unless we go to the library on the corner -- I usually do -- it's quieter there. Or on good days we play football in the courtyard. Then there's always some stupid chore to do before tea, or after -- we take turns..."

"I don't even get any tea. Mum is still out at work and if I go in the kitchen when my dad is home, he gives me a swat. But go on!"

"Well, after tea we usually play games or do puzzles, or homework..."

"At least I don't have to do homework. My folks couldn't care less." Bob's voice was cocky.

Anthony was a little shocked. Getting ahead in the world was very much stressed at Washburn.

"...and if there's a good program on, they let us watch television..."

"We had a telly, but my dad threw it out last month when something broke, and we haven't got another one yet. He goes to bed too early for the good programs, he says, and he doesn't want the thing on when he's trying to sleep." Bob shrugged. "We must be the only people in the world with no telly."

"Weekends we usually go somewhere special, us older ones, like to the park, or the zoo, or even out in the country."

Bob shrugged and scowled. "That's nuffing. I go all over London whenever I want."

Anthony heard the change in his tone and decided to change the subject. What could he say, to keep them friendly?

"I've run away before," he tried hopefully.

"What happened that time?" Their eyes glowed at him in the dim light from the street.

They were interested. All right, then. Anthony leaned back.

"I got this idea, see, about finding somebody that I looked like, and pretending I was a relative -- and I had to find a family where somebody had died just before I was born, to explain why they hadn't happened to hear about me before.

"That way, you see, I could pretend there was a secret marriage, and my mother died when I was born, and I just found out who my father was. I thought if I looked enough like the person who died, they wouldn't be able to turn me away. There are lots of books and magazines in the library, with pictures of rich people in them, so I started trying to find someone."

"Library?" It was obvious that none of the boys had ever before run into the thought that a library might be useful.

"Of course, I didn't care whether they were rich lords and ladies or not, but most of the books were about that kind, not about common ordinary people, so I thought, well, why not? So I aimed high -- too high, I suppose.

"There was an Earl of Moresby, who'd had a younger brother who had racing cars and was always getting into trouble and died when I was about a year old, so I just moved my birthday up a bit, to about six months after he died -- I'm small for my age, luckily..."

The boys laughed appreciatively.

"... and one fine day I left the orphan home and went to his house here in London. I went up to the door in my ragged old jumper and my cockney accent and asked boldly for the master, and the butler just shut the door in my face. Then I rang the bell again and said I was his lordship's nephew, and the butler said -- I'll never forget it -- he just said" (Anthony wiggled uneasily at the recollection) "'PREPOSTEROUS!' and shut the door again. So I just went back to the Home."

The boys leaned back. "Preposterous!" yelled Piggy, imitating Anthony's imitation of the butler.

"I'd have set fire to the house," muttered Donald, darkly.

"You're well out of it if it ended that way," said Bob. "Who'd want to live in a stuffy place like that?"

"Preposterous," agreed Piggy.

"I tried again," Anthony said, and the boys settled back.

"This time, it was just a baronet, Lord Orincourt, who has a place down in Kent. This time I had listened to the BBC for weeks, practicing a proper accent..." He began speaking with it, but had to stop when the boys started mimicking him grandly. When the good-natured laughter had died down, Anthony went on.

"I watched my manners more, too. The head matron didn't know what had come over me!"

Piggy stuck out his little finger and pretended to be drinking a cup of tea. Donald gave him a good-natured push.

"So by the time I got to Orincourt, I could have been an earl's son, or even a prince. I decided if I acted like a prince, people might take me for a lord, but if I acted like a lord, they might take me for a twit." More laughter.

"I went to Orincourt on a rainy day -- I had noticed a florist van that was sometimes at the market, from the same town, so I climbed in the back one day. I still had a long way to walk, and in the rain, to get to Orincourt. But I got there, and stood for hours peering through the gate, getting wetter and wetter, waiting.

"Finally my chance came. A girl came driving up in a sports car. Beautiful, she was, and I looked startled at her, but kept my hands on the bars of the gate. She smiled at me and asked if I'd open the gate for her, and I pretended to be in a sort of a daze and said, 'It looks different now -- the trees are bigger --' and looked back throught the gate again.

"So she got curious and asked me what I meant, and I said my mother had brought me there as a child to see the place and had said my father had lived there before he died, and then, so she wouldn't ask for too many details, I started to cry."

The boys nodded a bit shamefacedly, as though agreeing that, for once, that might be the thing to do.

"She took me into the house, and she and her brother, that was the baronet, kept asking me questions. I just tried to act like a prince, a tired one, and said I didn't know, it was so long ago I could hardly remember my mother, even.

"They fed me, and I thought I was getting somewhere, but then they phoned the police and found out I was from the Home, and that I'd never known my mother at all, so they told the police to come ahead and take me back to the Home."

"Coo," said Piggy. "Rotten luck."

"And now you're trying agin?" Bob shook his head. "You don't know when you're well off."

"You don't want to let toffs like that kick you about," Donald said, glowering. "We're as good as they are, my dad says."

"Aw, your Dad's a communist," Piggy said scathingly, and there was a scuffle that left them all panting.

"Come on, then," Bob said finally. "That lorry driver is leaving as soon as his mate shows up. You'll have to get hidden ahead of time, 'cause sometimes the mate sleeps in the back. Let's go take a look and see where we can put you."

The quarrel forgotten, the boys trooped out into the evening fog, and Anthony was guided through the lot and down the dimly-lit streets to an alley where the lorry was parked.

They climbed in and Bob lit a match to see what there was.

"You could hide behind them tarps," Piggy whispered.

"The mate might use them," Bob interrupted, holding his second match up high. "Look, there's kind of a bin along here for tools and that. If you got in there..." he yelped and dropped the match, stepping on it quickly. "We could cover you with one of the tarps, and then even if the mate did come back here, he'd not notice you -- at least not til daylight, and that's a long way off."

"You won't mind a belt or two at the end, as long as you get a good long ride, will you?" asked Donald.

Anthony shrugged. He'd never been belted before in his life, but he was sure he'd live through it.

The boys did their best to make sure he was hidden from sight, and finally, reluctantly, the boys left him to his adventure, wishing him luck.

Anthony smiled in the dark, thinking of the boys and wondering if he'd ever see them again. They were good fun. Maybe they could have come along... no, of course not. But it wasn't much fun being alone.

A soft rain began. Thankful for the shelter and lulled by the rhythmical pattering on the canvas roof, Anthony fell asleep.

C H A P T E R   6
****

Anthony awoke slowly, gradually realizing that the lorry had been moving for some time. Lights from passing cars swept by occasionally, and muffled voices could be heard through the partition that separated him from the driver's cab. Not far from him, an occasional snore told him that a third person was sleeping in the back.

"We have to," came emphatically through the partition.

Mumbled disgruntlement was the response. Anthony stretched himself cautiously.

"You can stay out of sight if you're worried." The Voice was patronizing and -- yes, oily was the word.

"What makes you think you'll get it?

"Don't make me laugh! You think I can't con a simple village maiden into giving us the key?"

"But Rundale said..."

"I know what Rundale said. He's too anxious. Arabella is the risk-taker of those two. She's got some guts. And she's told me to go ahead. It'll be easy. You'll see."

"Why are we going up so early, then? We aren't even doing the job until next week..."

"Stop grumbling, will you? I've got a little private business to attend to..." The voices died down to a mumble, and Anthony's eyes began to close again.

So they were on their way. Anthony had a sudden moment of doubt. Rob and Donald hadn't been all that certain the lorry was going to Yorkshire. What if he ended up in Cornwall?

For a moment, he considered trying to take a look outside, but decided it was too risky. After all, this was an adventure, getting out of London. Perhaps they would even get on the Dover ferry and go to France!

A picture of 15th century France rose before him, a scene from that film about Henry the Fifth. Banners and knights in armour, and swords and lances.

Not that that fit very well with the smell of machine oil and sweat and -- what was that other odor, bananas?

The man in the back rolled over, muttering, and Anthony held his breath. The man stumbled to his feet, swaying as the lorry rounded a curve. Anthony stiffened as the man came closer, leaned over, and banged on the partition.

"How about stopping for 'arf a mo..." He stopped in mid-shout as the lights from a passing car showed him Anthony. He stood with his mouth open while

Anthony, heart beating fast, prepared to leap out of the way.

They both moved together, the man shouting, as the lorry lumbered to a stop. Anthony wriggled out of his grasp and took a running leap out through the canvas back, rolling over on the roadway and then jumping to his feet and making for the woods in the wet fog.

He heard the driver shout, and the man he had struggled with called out, "There was a boy hiding in the back. Blimey, 'e gave me a turn."

"Do you think he heard anything?" asked the oily voice.

"What if 'e did? 'E's just one of them lads from my neighborhood. He'll have himself a time of it, getting home from 'ere!" The driver guffawed.

"Right, let's leave him to it, then."

Anthony, flat on the ground where he had tripped over a branch, listened with relief as the three men checked the tyres and then climbed back into the cab. The lorry rolled on.

With the lorry out of sight, Anthony picked himself up and made his way back to the road. He was already wet through, and muddy besides. He shivered, and began jogging along the road, trying to keep warm.

I wonder where I am, he thought. He could be just outside of London, for all he knew. Perhaps they hadn't gone very far.

The fog gave no indication of what time of night it might be. He squelched muddily along, trying to recapture his familiar dreams of a prince in disguise, cast from his rightful place by a terrible mistake. But it wasn't working.

He glanced fearfully toward the forest. He'd never been in a place so dark before -- London was always light enough to see where you were going. And the forest -- who knew what might be in a forest? He'd only visited one, by daylight, and even then there had been unfamiliar sounds.

A shape loomed at him from the fog, and he shied away, scalp prickling, before he realized it was only an old, dead tree trunk at a curve in the road.

He jogged a bit faster, but stumbled into the ditch, getting even muddier. He got up again and limped on, slower this time, slapping down his wet shoes noisily in order to discourage whatever it was that was making those rustling noises in the woods.

Sooner or later the road would have to come to a house or a village -- the forest couldn't go on forever -- and then what?

The road curved again, and with a feeling of great relief Anthony saw a light up ahead.

As he came closer, Anthony saw that it was a country inn, one of those ancient ones, with roses growing up the walls. A big lighted sign that said "Three Chimneys" hung by the road, lighting up an area of fog.

Anthony slowed to a stop, hesitating. He watched as the door opened and a man came out to sweep off the front step. He saw Anthony and nodded.

"Good morning, lad." He turned to go in again.

"Uh -- good morning -- could I --"

The man looked at him again.

"Do you suppose I c—could come in until the rain stops?"

"It may never stop, you know," the man said with a smile. "But you can come in and dry off, at least."

"Thank you." Anthony smiled with relief.

"Go round to the kitchen door, would you mind? Your shoes are muddy. Not your fault, but we just cleaned in here."

"Oh. All right." Anthony followed the man's pointing arm around to the left until he came to a door. He knocked hesitantly, and after a long minute the man opened the door and jerked his head for Anthony to enter.

At the end of a small passageway, they came into a large and cheery kitchen, where a large and cheery woman was working at putting breakfast on several trays.

The man eyed Anthony thoughtfully. "You running away from home?"

Anthony's jaw dropped. Was it that obvious?

"From an orphan's home, sir." Anthony knew he was playing for sympathy, and hurried on. "I'm trying to find my uncle."

"I see. You sure you haven't got a Mum at home worrying about you?"

"No, sir. Wish I had."

"Well, get that muddy jacket off and let Millie clean it up for you. Looks like you fell in a ditch." He picked up a tray and hesitated for a moment.

"We're short-handed here today," he said brusque-
ly. "My nephew's in London and Betsy's out sick. If
you want to lend us a hand, just for the day, you can
have a night's lodging, your meals, and a pound or two
to help you on your way. What do you say?"

Anthony's mouth dropped open again and then
turned into a huge grin. "Yes, SIR!"

"Well then. Mind you don't drop anything. Take
a tray in to grandfather in there, would you? And get
another for yourself. Eat with him, he likes company.
I'll lead the way."

Anthony carefully picked up a tray of food and
followed to a small room off the hall.

"Grandfather" was hoisting himself up in his bed,
his white hair sticking up in sleepy points.

"Hello there," the old man said with a smile.
"Where did you come from?"

"I'm just passing through." Anthony laid the
tray on the man's lap.

"Passing through, eh? That's a good one. You
tell Charlie you're going to eat in here with me, will
you?"

Anthony smiled. "He already suggested that, sir.
Just let me get my tray."

"Call me Pops," the old man called after him as
Anthony went out the door.

"Now then," said Pops as Anthony returned and sat
down with the tray on his knees. "What's your name,
and where are you from?"

"I'm Anthony, and I'm from London." Anthony
looked at his breakfast hungrily. Bacon, eggs, a

stewed tomato, sausage, porridge, toast and tea. A feast!

"I got a ride here in a lorry, and I don't even know where this is," he added as they both started to eat. "How far is it from London?"

"About 200 miles, lad. We're near to Selby.'"

"Is that far from York?"

"Oh dear no. Only 15 miles or so."

Anthony brightened. That was good news.

"You running away from home, are you?" Pops asked casually, piling up the back of his fork with bacon and egg.

"Not exactly. I'm just sort of going visiting."

Pops chuckled and shook his head, and Anthony grinned back.

"I ran away to sea, myself, once, when I wasn't much older than you."

Anthony looked at the old man with interest. "Are you close to the sea, here?"

Pops gave a snort. "Not very -- that's maybe why I fell in love with it, first time I saw it."

"I've been to the seaside on holidays, sometimes, but it always seemed to be stormy when we were there."

"Aye, it was the storms drove me back home again. I found out I get seasick. But I got as far as Rio and back."

Anthony's eyes shone. Rio! It sounded exciting, and exotic, and unimaginably far away. "I'd like to go there some day," he said recklessly.

"No doubt." Pops was silent for a while, eating his toast and marmalade. "But I found out home was a pretty interesting place, too," he went on, finally. "Plenty of secrets in this old inn."

"Secrets?"

"Certainly. This room you're sitting in now was a secret room for more than 300 years -- and that staircase in the corner led to two more secret rooms upstairs. Nobody knew about them except our family, oldest son to oldest son."

Anthony looked at the circular stone steps with interest. "How did -- what did..."

"Ah. Well, I'll begin at the beginning. Our name is Stoner. A Stoner built this house, back in 1469. There have been Stoners here ever since, which is a good record, don't you think?

"Old Robert Stoner, the builder, he was a fine mason -- worked on castles and churches all over Britain, and his seven sons worked with him. He specialized in secret rooms. It's a family story that old Robert said there wasn't an earl or a bishop in the country that didn't have something to hide!

"Of course, in those days, when noblemen just weren't happy unless they had some feud or plot going on, it was useful to have a place nobody else knew about. Anyway, a grateful patron finally gave old Robert this bit of land, and he and his sons built this house for Robert to retire to. He'd built so many secret rooms and passages and listening holes, he decided to build some into his own house, just in case.

"But he never got a chance to enjoy the house. He went off to build one last castle, and never came

back. Fell off a roof, so they said. So the oldest
son inherited the property, and so on right down to
me. Charlie's next in line, and then unless he and
Millie get busy and have some babes, it'll go to
Bert."

Anthony spread marmalade on his third piece of
toast. "Did the secret rooms ever hide anybody, or
any treasure?"

"When Bloody Mary was Queen, they did -- and
again in Cromwell's time -- there were some Quakers
hidden here, to escape going to prison, though I never
quite saw what difference it made. I mean, they were
locked up here, too, weren't they?

"Then in the 1700's the place became an inn, and
it was awkward, getting food from the kitchen way
around to the public room in there, so my great-
grandfather had the bright idea of knocking a
passageway through here and opening up the secret
rooms. Pity, in a way, I always thought."

"How did people used to get into the room,
before?"

"That over there was a solid wall, on the public
rooms side, and it just looked like part of the fireplace wall. On the kitchen side, though, there was a
big square cupboard, like. There was some way to
unlock it, and then you had to climb into the cupboard
and push at the back, so they say. I'm afraid no one
knows any more how it worked. But it was pretty
ingenious, eh? They used to use this room for private
parties, but a few years back I decided I'd had enough
of stairs, so I moved in here, myself. The staff

rooms are upstairs there, so we can come down early without disturbing the guests."

The kitchen door opened just then, and Charlie poked his head in.

"If you're through with breakfast, lad, we could use you." He disappeared again.

Anthony hastily stuffed in the last of the toast and grabbed up the tray. "I'll come back later, if I can."

"Good. Here, you can take my tray, too. Just put it on top, like this."

Anthony took the two trays, which were less wobbly than he had supposed, and backed out the door. His first day as a working man was about to begin.

CHAPTER 7
****

In the big public room, with its dark beams, huge fireplace, and white-washed walls, the boarders were eating breakfast. The fog was lifting, and there was a pale light beginning to show in the sky. Some big windows at the end of the room looked out across the moors, where only a few sheep moved.

Anthony brought in the toast, while Charlie poured more tea. Millie was kept busy in the kitchen.

A big fat man with a tea towel tucked under his chin, shoveled food into his mouth in a methodical rhythm. Over by the window a man with a mustache drank tea absent-mindedly, staring out at the moors while his eggs grew cold. At another table all that was visible was a newspaper, held up in full spread by a pair of pudgy hands. There were three middle-aged couples, too, all of them looking sleepy and not talking much.

When they had gone, he helped Millie with the washing up, while Charlie carried in trays of dishes. Then Anthony wiped off the tables and swept the floor.

The next job was helping make beds and straighten rooms upstairs, as the boarders drifted out for the day. It was a big place, and obviously a busy one, even though it was out here in the country.

Millie liked singing, and taught Anthony "Ilka Moor" as they worked together:

"Where hast tha been since I saw thee?

On Ilka Moor bar t'at..."

"What's bar t'at mean?" Anthony asked.

"Without a hat," Millie said, ruffling his hair. "We'll have you speaking Yorkshire in no time at all."

After an 11 o'clock cup of tea, Charlie took Anthony with him in the van to shop in Selby, and Anthony was kept busy carrying packages. Charlie pointed out Selby Abbey, and Anthony, remembering Westminster, wondered if Marc Elliot had ever been there. He had asked about being a Yorkist...

"Did Robert Stoner build this abbey?" Anthony turned to ask Charlie.

"I see Pops has been telling you our history already." Charlie laughed. "He worked on part of it -- see that big window over the entrance? And also on what is now the vestry, around on the other side. But most of the Abbey is a lot older than Robert Stoner. It was started in the 1100's. See the main door, there? That kind of door, with a round arch and that sort of decoration, that's always Norman work, before 1200. Unless it's a copy, of course."

"How can you tell where Robert Stoner worked, after all this time?"

"First, it's a family tradition. Second -- ever heard of mason's marks?"

Anthony shook his head.

"Masons in the old days each had a special mark, that they put on all the stones they worked, and that's how they were paid, by how many stones had their mark on them. I'll show you Robert Stoner's mark when we get home. It's almost like what our family always called a 'Jerusalem cross.' I never heard anyone else call it that, though. It's like -- well, I'll show you when we get back home."

Back at the inn, Charlie forgot. Anthony unloaded the van, set up the dining room for lunch, and then ate in the kitchen with Pops.

"Well, lad, glad to see you back again. Charlie isn't working you too hard, is he? You just tell me, if he is. Did you see our famous abbey when you were in town?"

"Yes. Oh -- Charlie told me he'd show me Robert Stoner's mason's mark."

"Oh yes!" Pops looked pleased. "Come on, I'll show you."

He led Anthony over to the big kitchen fireplace, and poked with a poker at a stone just inside it, under the mantelpiece.

"There now. Take a look."

Anthony peered inside. Sure enough, there on the stone, much blackened with soot, but unmistakable, was a cross with a short, perpendicular line at the end of each crosspiece, except at the top.

Anthony felt it with his fingers. Five hundred years old was pretty old.

They went back to their lunch. "Could I see what beer tastes like?" Anthony asked as he picked up his knife and fork. He looked curiously at the foaming mug in front of Millie.

"Well now." Pops scratched his chin, where he had missed a bit of beard in his shaving. "You wouldn't want us to lose our license, would you? Anyway, you don't want to start down that road. Why, this house almost got stopped before it was finished, all because of strong drink."

Anthony grinned at him unbelievingly. "But this is a pub!"

"It's true, though. It seems that Robert's father, old Archibald, was a monumental drinker, and he wanted his son to build a good wine cellar under the house. Naturally, that was the first thing finished. In those days, you know, the wine came in big barrels, and they were put up on big cross-pieces, like an X, so you could draw wine from the spigot more easily.

"Old Archibald began a practice of starting at one end of the barrels and taking a glass of wine from each. He started calling it 'The Way of the Cross,' which nearly got him ex-communicated -- a serious business in those days. The Bishop of York happened along one day when Archy was doing his perambulation, and if it hadn't been for Robert coming along in the nick of time and giving the Bishop a large donation, who knows what would have happened? Archy was shipped back to London to get him out of Robert's hair -- and most of the wine cellar went with him."

"Are you still letting our family skeletons out of the closet?" Millie had come by in time to hear the last bit.

"I like hearing about families," Anthony said, and then blushed slightly, knowing he was playing for sympathy again.

"You mentioned an uncle, didn't you? Does he live in York?" Millie brought her tea cup over and sat down with them.

"Ye-es, well, Yorkshire. I'm not sure he would be able to take me in, but I thought I'd try."

"That's the spirit. Can't win by not trying, can you! But come on, the two of you are finished -- how about doing some of the dishes while I go have a lie down and rest my feet?"

After the dishes, there was silver to polish, woodwork to wash, the floor to sweep. Then it was tea-time again, and another quiet meal with Pops, who told him some stories about when he was a boy.

"That time I ran away to sea, it was summer." He gave Anthony a quick glance from under his bushy eyebrows. "It took a while to find a ship, but I could sleep out in the fields, and live on berries, that time of year. Even then, I got lonesome for human company pretty quick."

"I know it's not a good time of year, but -- I'll be too big pretty soon. I thought -- while I'm small --"

"You'd have a better chance, eh? You may be right."

"Yes, sir."

"Where you were -- I'll bet it wasn't all that bad, what do you say?"

Anthony thought of Bob and Piggy, and sighed. "Perhaps not. But I'd just like --" he paused, wondering how often he had said it before -- "to be in a real family, where everyone cares about each other."

Pops nodded. "Well, I wish you luck, lad. Let me know what happens, will you?"

"All right, Pops."

"Hmph. I wondered when you were going to stop calling me 'sir'! Anyway, don't you worry. A fine, helpful boy like you should be welcome any place. Don't you forget that."

Anthony blushed, and started picking up the dishes. "Thank you, Pops," he mumbled, and went back to work.

Then it was evening, and the bar started to get busy. Charlie wouldn't let Anthony go into the public room once the bar was opened up, but he was allowed to sit in Pops' room and listen as Millie played the piano and everyone sang.

Then Bert came back from London and started playing his guitar. It was jolly, but eventually Anthony's eyes began to droop.

I sure wouldn't want to run an inn if the working day is this long, he thought. And then everyone gets up early to start breakfast!

Millie led him up the old secret stairs to Bert's room, one of the rooms that had once been hidden. She gave him a toothbrush from their small shop, and turned down one of the twin beds.

"Here's one of Bert's pajama tops for you -- he never wears one, anyway. Sleep well, love." She gave him a quick kiss, which made his heart give a funny kind of leap, and left him to get ready for bed.

He stood for a moment, looking around the cozy room. Maybe if things didn't work out at Rothwick Castle... He got undressed, smiling to himself, and climbed into bed. He turned out the light and lay in the dark, listening to the faint sounds of music and laughter from below, and glowing with a warm feeling inside, before falling asleep.

In the morning, noises from the kitchen woke him. Bert had already dressed and gone, so Anthony jumped up and dressed quickly. Down in the bustling kitchen, he saw a new face -- that must be Betsy, recovered. Bert was there, and Charlie and Millie greeted Anthony warmly and set out his breakfast. His jacket, clean and dry, was waiting for him, too. Anthony joined Pops at the table for another huge breakfast.

He ate slowly, feeling a little lost, and wishing that -- no, he shouldn't wish to stay here. He should go and see Rothwick, at least, since he was this close. And then -- then maybe he should go back to Washburn Home for Boys.

Anyway, he couldn't work at Three Chimneys all the time, he knew that. He wasn't old enough, and besides, he'd have to go to school, and then what use would he be? But it had been fun to help, he thought wistfully.

As he reluctantly finished off the last of the toast, Charlie came over and sat down with a cup of tea.

"We'll pack you a good lunch," he said, "and here's a fiver. You were a real help yesterday."

A whole five pounds! Anthony beamed at him. "Thank you very much!"

"Wouldn't want you to go hungry. I'll put you on the road to York, if you like, when I go in to Selby this morning. I'll be leaving in a few minutes."

"I'm ready," Anthony said, patting the toothbrush in his pocket.

"You do travel light, for a fact!" Millie called across the kitchen, and they all laughed.

"Come back, if you don't find what you want in York," Charlie said gruffly, and strode off to get his coat. Anthony fought back sudden tears. He really did have a chance to stay at Three Chimneys. Maybe he wouldn't have to go back to Washburn after all!

"Here, lad, you might be glad of a cap in this kind of weather." Pops handed him a knitted ski cap, and Anthony pulled it on.

"Wouldn't want you to be out on Ilka Moor bar t'at," Betsy said.

"That used to be Bert's, but he's got a swelled head now, it don't fit any more," Millie joked. She came over to give Anthony a quick goodbye kiss.

That was twice, Anthony thought, glowing inside.
Maybe he didn't **always** have to pretend his mother was
a duchess. Maybe she could be like Millie.

They waved goodbye as he climbed into the van.
As they pulled away from Three Chimneys, Anthony
looked back and sighed.

In Selby, Charlie found a friend who was going to
York, and put Anthony in his care. They made several
deliveries on the way, and it was nearly lunchtime
before they reached Micklegate Bar, one of the ancient
entries to the city of York.

As they crossed the Ouse, the driver pointed to
where the great towers of York Minster rose above the
city.

The van stopped near the Shambles, and Anthony,
thanking the man for the ride, got down and stared
about him. There were lots of people strolling about,
looking in the shop windows, more like at a carnival
than in a city. The streets were narrow, but everything seemed to be painted white, so it was light and
clean-looking. Some of the upper storeys hung out
over the street, which made it seem cozy and friendly.

Anthony stopped to look in an antique shop window,
and spotted a brass Beefeater with a spike in his
hand. The Washburn boys had often been taken to visit
the Tower of London, where the Beefeaters in their red
and gold uniforms were great favorites. They told the
boys all about the beheadings. For a moment, the
brass statue made Anthony feel homesick for London.

He wandered down the Petergate, toward the
cathedral, but then spotted the city walls, where one

or two people were walking, and decided to go there.
He was a little afraid of being noticed in the street
on a school day.

The walls were ancient, and Anthony began thinking again about Richard of York. He must have been
here, he thought, looking down on these same streets,
that same Minster. It was as good a territory as
London had always been, for providing scenes for his
pretendiing.

He sat down on the wall, at a point where he
could look across the city streets, and took out his
lunch. There was a flash of blue, and a tiny
chaffinch flew close, puffing out its rosy chest and
cocking a beady black eye at him. Anthony threw it
some crumbs, pleased to have such company.

A noise below him at Bootham Bar scared the
chaffinch away, and Anthony climbed up to look over
the wall. A lorry had broken down, causing something
of a traffic jam. Three men were pushing the lorry
out of the way while horns beeped and a few drivers
shouted. Then the driver got out of the cab and opened
the hood.

Anthony was about to jump down again when he
heard a familiar, oily voice.

"This is a fine fix you've got us into."

Then it clicked. That was the lorry he had
ridden up in from London! He looked at the men more
curiously. The one who had been in the back, asleep,
must be the short, stocky one -- Anthony recognized
the shoulders under the brown tweed jacket. The
driver would be the quick nervous one, smoking a

cigarette with short, angry puffs as he leaned against the radiator.

It was the third man, the one who seemed to be their leader, that Anthony was most curious about, but he was facing the other way. Anthony could only see his black, wavy hair stirring in the breeze, above the collar of his sheepskin jacket. But the voice was unmistakable.

"It's your job to provide the lorry," he was saying coldly. "You'd better see to it that it's back running again, and soon." He swore. "Good job we DID come up early, in spite of all your complaints. Now get moving."

Anthony smiled to himself. Served them right! He turned to jump down.

"I say, look where you're going, will you?"

Anthony grinned at the boy he had almost jumped onto, a freckle-faced redhead. "Sorry," he said. Then he looked again. "No school today?" he asked cautiously.

"No, Bootham's on holiday this week."

"Bootham?" Anthony looked blank.

"The school. You know. Surely you've heard of it?"

Anthony shook his head. "I'm from London."

"Oh. What school are you in, then?"

Anthony realized the boy was talking about posh schools, and was assuming, because of Anthony's new school blazer, that he attended one, too.

"Washburn Academy," Anthony invented.

"Now we're even. I never heard of yours, either." The boy smiled, and Anthony relaxed. If some of the schools were on holidays, he needn't be afraid to wander about.

"Where's Bootham?"

The boy pointed. "Over that way."

"Oh, here in York?

The boy shook his head in disgust. "These foreigners from London!"

Anthony changed the subject. He still wanted to see the cathedral. "I was about to go and see the Minster. Want to come along?"

"All right. If you've never been, I'll be your guide."

"Just so long as you don't expect to get paid!" They laughed, and went down the steps to street level.

"I haven't seen any other boys about," Anthony said, still curious.

"Most of them have gone home, of course."

"But you live in York?"

The boy made a face. "No, Northumberland. If you must know, my parents don't want me at home, so I'm staying over. They're having house guests, and I 'wouldn't fit in,' so it's either staying here or going to my aunt's, which is far, far worse. I love York, and it's nice to have time to roam around without being herded in a group."

"I know what you mean," Anthony managed to stammer, still in shock to think that the boy's parents wouldn't want him at home.

They stepped inside the cool cathedral, automatically speaking more quietly.

Anthony hesitated in front of a sign that asked for donations, and the boy said quickly, "I'll put something in for both of us. At least I've always got plenty of money."

"I've only got a five-pound note, and I don't really want to put all that in," Anthony said apologetically.

"It's all right. Come on."

They wandered up the nave, Anthony still puzzling over the fact that a boy could have parents and still not be close to them. I've never been able to think about perhaps not being wanted, it hurt too much, he thought. But this chap KNOWS he's not wanted, and doesn't seem to care that much.

"Wouldn't you rather be at home?" he asked tentatively as they poked down the aisles, looking at the effigies.

"What? Oh, I don't know. I've been away at school since I was eight --" (another shock for Anthony) "-- and it isn't all that much fun at home, anyway. I'm used to being on my own." But there was hurt in his voice, Anthony could hear it.

He was silent, his throat aching. Perhaps this boy and he were from different kinds of homes, but they had something in common.

"Here, look at this." The other boy had paused in front of a glass case. "This is what the City of York said when Richard the Third died: 'to the great

heaviness of this city...' Doesn't sound as if he was
so hated as Henry Tudor tried to make out, does it!"

"Are you a Friend of Richard III, too?"

The boy looked pleased. "So you know about that,
even down in London? Yes, my family belongs. I've
been almost everywhere that was connected with Richard
-- Middleham, Richmond, Raby -- even Sheriff Hutton,
where his son was buried. I felt very sorry for
Richard when I saw that pathetic little tomb. And of
course, Leicester, where he was taken after he was
killed at Bosworth. There's a plaque on Bow Bridge,
showing where his body was thrown into the river."

"Seriously? They threw a king in the river?"

The boy shrugged. "Tudor's claim to the throne
was pretty shaky. He needed the excuse that Richard
was a tyrant and a usurper. A thoroughly bad lot,
Tudor."

They finished their perambulation of the Minster
and went out again into the October sunshine.

Anthony looked up at the sun. "Afraid I have to
be on my way," he said. "It was nice meeting you.
I'm Anthony..." he hesitated over his last name, suddenly realizing that he might have been mentioned in
the news as "missing."

"I'm Paul Forbes. Come and visit Bootham
sometime. It's not a bad place, as schools go."

"I will," Anthony said somewhat uncomfortably,
sorry now that he hadn't been honest, had pretended to
be a from a posh school.

Paul headed down the Shambles and Anthony turned
toward the road to Scarborough. Whenever he heard a

lorry coming, he turned and put out a surreptitious thumb. He walked for what seemed a long time, but finally, as houses started thinning out and the countryside emerged, a lorry stopped.

He got a short ride, then another, then a third, explaining to each curious driver that he hadn't enough money for the bus. (The five pounds didn't count -- that was his life savings!)

The day had been growing darker and colder, with black clouds scudding furiously along in the high wind, and when Anthony finally descended at the tiny road at which a weathered signpost pointed to "Nether Rothwick," he was glad for the cap Pops had given him.

Shivering, he watched as the lorry drove out of sight, leaving him alone on the deserted country road.

C H A P T E R   8
****

Anthony looked around him, curious, but also afraid. There wasn't a house in sight. Rows of twisted trees separated one scrubby field from another, across desolate-looking hills. Anthony buttoned his jacket and thrust his hands in his pockets, feeling cold and very alone. This was certainly different from London!

Then he turned, reluctantly, to the Rothwick road, which wandered off among the bleak hills.

Well, he thought. Now I need you, Richard the Third. He squared his shoulders. I'm as good as anybody, he thought. He started off down the road, whistling for confidence until the sharp wind forced him to stop.

He walked for what seemed like miles without seeing anyone, only an occasional lapwing circling curiously over him, calling its loud "Pit-wee."

Ahead, the road ran through a forest. He hung back, cautious of its darkness, until he thought of Robin Hood and his merry men. He found a stick that would serve as a staff, and strode on as if he were Will Scarlett.

At the other edge of the forest, he stopped and stared. There, just across a stretch of meadow, were the towers of a castle. Rothwick!

Without even thinking, he ducked into the shelter of the trees, not ready to be seen. With thumping heart he stared at the castle.

It wasn't huge, like Hampton Court, but it looked pretty solid. There were two square towers, with a main gate between. Looked as if there must have been a moat there once, but it had been filled in. Over the huge door was a coat of arms worked in stone.

Anthony's mouth felt dry. Here he was -- he had made it -- but he was ready to turn and run. How could he possibly approach such a place? How had he ever imagined he could?

Maybe he had already grown up too much, and no longer had that innocence about people and families that had led him on his earlier adventures.

Still, he might as well look the place over. Cautiously, still keeping in the shadow of the forest, he started making his way up the hill.

The west side of the castle had some larger windows, and another entrance. A handcart was leaning against the wall by the door, and some smoke rose lazily from one of the chimneys.

For the first time, it occurred to Anthony that perhaps there might not have been anyone there. Earls and such probably went to Greece for the winter. Then what would he have done?

In fact, what was he to do now? It was nearly sunset, and it was cold. Nobody at a castle was going to let a strange boy in to spend the night, he realized that now.

Anthony bit his lip, feeling his courage sliding away. "Be not afraid?" Easier said than done.

He crept slowly on up the hill, through the pines and oaks, stealing glances at the forbidding-looking castle and wondering whether he shouldn't just go right back to Three Chimneys.

He was so busy staring at the castle, he didn't notice at first that there was someone else at the forest edge. It was a woman, who sat painting at an easel.

He stopped, and crouched low, but she hadn't heard him, over the sound of the wind in the trees. His heart lifted a little, remembering Marc's friendliness, and he decided there was nothing lost if he approached her.

He got close enough to see the picture she was working on. Yes, she was doing the castle, but adding a tournament in the field.

"I say, that's awfully good," he blurted out.

The artist leaped up, startled. "What? Who are you? What are you doing here?" She snatched up her painting and turned it away from him.

"I don't allow people to watch me painting," she said, looking cross and upset. "Please go away."

Anthony tried to divert her. "I know another artist. Want to see the picture he drew of me?" He reached into his pocket.

"No indeed!" The woman looked around as if for help. "I mean -- I'm sorry, but I don't talk to strange boys. And you shouldn't be here. This is our private property." She snapped shut her artist's case, wrestled the old easel under her arm, and almost ran away from him, towards the castle.

"You'd better go home!" drifted back as she went.

Anthony watched her go for a long moment, the sketch still in his hand.

She was going to the castle. His heart sank. Would she be the countess, then? Lady Daphne? "Our property," she had said. His heart sank some more.

He looked down at his picture, and carefully started folding it up. Well, that's that, he thought. Ended before it even started. Anyway, she isn't at ALL like...

He could feel the tears begin to smart behind his eyes, and for once did nothing to stop them. There was no one there to see. All his long travels suddenly caught up with him, and he couldn't manage any more to pretend that he was a prince, or that anyone would ever care about him.

He threw himself down on the bed of oak leaves and let some of his disappointment out in a few sobs. Then, feeling ashamed of himself, he rolled over on his back.

To his astonishment, he encountered another pair of eyes, peering at him with some concern from the tree above him. He hastily drew his sleeve across his wet face, and then looked up again, warily.

"Don't mind her," said a voice. "She's like that with everybody."

Anthony couldn't answer.

"There's a good view of the castle from up here. You can come up if you want."

Anthony lay still for another minute, wondering whether to respond or run. But what difference did it make, now, if someone had seen him cry? Anyway, they hadn't mentioned it.

He stood up, brushing off the leaves, and swung himself up the tree.

The oak still had plenty of leaves on it, even if they were brown and curling up. It made a good hiding place.

"Why, you're a girl!" Anthony had reached the spot where the voice was coming from. Seeing the girl start to scowl, he went on hurriedly, "This is almost like a tree house."

The girl looked at him for a moment, and then her face cleared. "Yes, I come up here a lot. Look, you can see the sea over there, between those hills."

They were silent for a moment, looking out across the moors, past the chimneys of a village he could now see in a hollow beyond the castle, to the glimpse of sea. Then they turned to look each other over. The girl was about Anthony's age, with plain brown hair, cut short; gray eyes, and a sullen-looking mouth.

"Was that -- was that the countess?"

"Yes." The girl giggled. "I had an awful time being quiet -- I knew she'd go mad if she knew anyone was watching. Sorry I couldn't warn you."

"That's all right."

"Can I see your drawing?"

Anthony took the picture out again, and unfolded it carefully.

"That's really good!" The girl glanced at him as if checking its accuracy. "Who's Marcus Elliot?"

"An artist I met in London."

"London? Is that where you're from? But -- where are you staying?"

"I don't know, I just got here."

She stared at him with a puzzled frown. "Where are your parents, then?"

"Haven't got any."

"Don't be silly. What do you mean?"

"Seek not to know, fair damsel. I come from another world."

She smiled briefly, as if to humor him, and then looked at him accusingly.

"I think you've run away from home."

"From an orphan's home. That's not so bad, is it?"

"No, I suppose not." She turned her head to stare at the castle. "I've thought about running away, but I'd never manage it. But you didn't come all the way from London, surely? Where do you sleep at night? It's getting cold."

"I slept in a lorry the first night, and some people gave me a bed last night, but I don't know about tonight. This tree might be a good place."

She turned to look at him again, and twisted her lip in her fingers.

"You hungry? I am. Come on, I'll tell my mother I've invited you to tea. And maybe with any luck she'll let you spend the night." She began dropping nimbly down from branch to branch.

Anthony brightened. That was the best he could hope for, and he was grateful. At least he'd have a chance to eat, and get warm. He'd think about tomorrow later.

He followed her down, and she led the way out into the field toward the village. But no, she was leading him toward the castle!

He stopped, his heart beating painfully, and she stopped, too.

"You live -- there?" He gestured with his chin, his hands pushed deep in his pockets.

"Come on, it's all right. Mother isn't really as bad as she sounded. She never lets anyone see her paintings, even us. Please don't let on that I was watching, too!" She giggled.

Anthony started walking slowly on again, his mind whirling.

"Did you really think it was good?"

"Huh? Oh, your mother's painting? Sure, didn't you?"

"I liked it, but I didn't know if it was any good. My father's always telling us how ignorant we are. He's an art expert, himself," she added with some pride.

They approached the door at the side of the castle. The girl paused. "I'm Elaine, by the way. And you're Anthony, right?"

"How did -- oh, from the drawing!" Anthony grinned. "You're a pretty good detective."

She smiled, pleased, and pushed open the heavy door.

Anthony looked past her into a dark hallway. Rothwick Castle -- and he wasn't going to have to storm the walls with his knights after all, he was being invited to tea! What would Gerry think of him now?

His heart still thumping against his green pullover, he took a deep breath and stumbled after the girl, into Rothwick Castle.

C H A P T E R   9
****

The door banged shut behind them, and Anthony
paused to let his eyes adjust to the dark. Elaine was
already moving ahead, and opened the door to a kitchen. Anthony followed, thinking desperately, "I'm
not ready for this -- I'm just not ready."

An older girl was stirring something on the
cooker.

"Diana, this is my friend Anthony. He's staying
for tea." Elaine poked her nose into the pot. "Not
Brussels sprouts again!"

"If you don't like my cooking, how about YOU
doing it, then?" Diana slammed the lid down.

"Oh well, if you're in a bad mood, we'll leave."

Elaine pulled Anthony with her out into the hall,
past a winding stone staircase, and through another
door into the main entryway, where Anthony looked with
interest at the inside of the massive front door, with
its carvings and brass studs. Then they turned
through the door opposite it, into a high-ceilinged
Great Hall like the one the Washburn boys had been

taken to visit last year. There was even some of that carved oak furniture that Anthony had liked.

The countess was kneeling at the great fireplace, rolling up newspapers. "Is that you, Elaine? I did ask you not to let the fire go out..." she began crossly, but stopped, startled, as she looked up and saw Anthony.

"Mother, this is my friend Anthony. I've invited him for tea." Elaine's belligerent formality seemed to erase any objections.

After hesitating a moment, looking distracted, the woman turned back to the fire. "That's nice, dear." Anthony noticed he was holding his breath, and let it out slowly.

"Perhaps the two of you wouldn't mind fetching some more wood."

"Why should I have to? I have a guest. Let Beth do it."

Much to Anthony's surprise, Elaine's mother said nothing to this. Anthony had opened his mouth to say he'd be glad to go, but Elaine was already pulling him out of the hall.

"Come on, I'll show you my room," she said, and ran up the stairs.

Anthony followed more slowly, his mind in a whirl. What a strange family this was!

At the top of the stairs another girl stood looking down at him haughtily, and Anthony stopped, looking up at her.

"Well? What are you staring at?"

"You're just fishing for a compliment," Elaine said crossly. "We all know you're the beauty of the family. Just go beautify some other corner of the house. Anthony's MY guest."

The beautiful but cool green eyes swept him up and down with calculated scorn, and Anthony felt embarrassment rising redly into his face.

"How d'you do. I'm Lady Elizabeth."

Elaine hooted. "You're Lady Impossible! Come on, Anthony."

Elizabeth turned and flounced down the stairs, sweeping grandly past Anthony, her honey-blonde hair bouncing at her back.

Elaine led the way down a corridor and into a large and rather gloomy room. "Sorry it's so cold in here. Daddy doesn't let us heat our bedrooms; he says it's bad for the health, but it's really because we haven't got much money."

Anthony stared at her. Could an earl with a castle be poor? But would a countess be setting her own fire, while her daughter cooked in the kitchen and another daughter fetched the wood?

"We haven't got much stuff up here, either, it's mostly down in London," Elaine was saying.

"London! What's it doing there?"

"We live there, unfortunately. This is just our October break from school. We'll be going back again on Sunday."

Anthony bit his lip. So he had come all this way when he could just as easily have met them in London!

He smiled ruefully. Well, he'd enjoyed the trip, anyway.

Elaine had turned sympathetic again, misinterpreting his expression. "Perhaps we can come and visit you when we're all back there," she said kindly.

Anthony turned to look out the window. Oh, fine, just like all those other visitors with their pity and their distance and their superior airs.

"I'm not going back," he said, but his heart wasn't in it. He was feeling very tired.

A bell rang downstairs.

"Time for tea." Elaine looked at him uncertainly.

Anthony roused himself with an effort, and gave her a smile. "Let's go, then."

Tea was not a happy occasion. Elaine and Beth quarreled fiercely over who was going to do the dishes, while Diana and her mother sat in silence, their thoughts obviously withdrawn to some separate, secret place.

Anthony did his best to play peacemaker, offering to do the dishes himself, and trying to divert the conversation, but with little success.

When he again mentioned the artist he'd met at Westminster, the countess blushed faintly and looked contrite.

"Perhaps you'd -- like to show us the picture he drew for you,'" she said with difficulty.

Anthony handed it over silently, feeling some

reluctance and resentment. At least she studied it
for a flatteringly long time.

"Marcus Elliot," she read softly, almost to herself. "He's very well known. And should be. He's
good." She sighed, staring at the quick sketch. "That
eagerness of boyhood," she murmured to herself. "And
something else -- wistfulness -- he's caught it all
very well..."

She glanced at him, and Anthony, surprised, saw
that her gray eyes were now looking at him with sympathy. With horror, he remembered he'd been crying.
Were there tear-stains on his face? His hand flew up
to rub his cheeks.

She was still staring at him, with a strange sort
of interest. Anthony could feel the blood rising in
his face.

She shook herself suddenly, as if aware that
she'd been staring. "I've never done a portrait," she
said. "Would you sit for me, Anthony? I'd like to
give it a try."

There was a sudden fascinated silence as her
three daughters stared at her, and then at Anthony.

She's trying to apologize, thought Anthony in
surprise, and felt touched by it. "I'd like that. All
right."

"Why not let Anthony spend the night, then you
can work on it tomorrow morning when the light's just
right?" Elaine spoke in a rush.

"Spend the night! What would his parents say?"

Elaine hesitated, and looked over at Anthony.

"I haven't any parents. I've run away from an orphan's home in London."

"Dear me!" They all looked at him with renewed interest. "All the way from London! But they'll be worrying about you! We must let them know where you are."

"Mother, please, shouldn't we wait until Daddy comes back?" Elaine crossed her fingers, and held them below table level for Anthony to see. "He'll know what to do. And the phone isn't connected."

"Well --" the countess's eyes wavered. "I suppose that's the best thing."

"Oh good, Anthony! That means you can stay at least until Saturday!"

"And perhaps you can go back to London with us," said Diana, trying to be helpful.

Anthony made no reply to that, but his heart was racing again. This was Monday -- he'd be with them for practically a whole week, if all went well. It would at least be a visit to remember!

"Th-thanks," he managed to stammer, and the countess lowered her eyes, looking a bit frightened.

"Won't -- won't Daddy disapprove?" asked Beth.

"What difference will it make -- he disapproves of everything already," Elaine said, frowning.

"I'll write and tell him before he arrives," the countess said. "You'd better write to the Home, too, Anthony, first thing in the morning."

She glanced again at the sketch Elliot had done, before handing it back. "This is quite good, Anthony. I'll find you something to keep it in, to protect it."

"Was it really awful at the orphan's home, like Oliver Twist?" Elizabeth asked, her green eyes looking less cool.

"Not really, I just..."

"Just what?"

"...want to live in a real family, where -- where everyone cares about each other." The old familiar words seemed to stick in his throat. **This** family didn't seem to care. Could he have been wrong about what families were like? Were they no better than the Home, after all? His heart sank.

He glanced around the table, but everyone's head was down; he couldn't tell what they might be thinking.

Diana got up and started clearing away the dishes, and Anthony got up to help, too. In the end, Elaine came grumblingly along, and the three did the dishes out in the kitchen. Casting about for a way to break the silence, Anthony remembered Millie at Three Chimneys, and began singing "Ilka Moor." The girls joined in, and Anthony grinned at them happily.

After that, the washing up went swiftly and didn't seem like work, although Elaine looked as if she'd never admit it.

The girls' mother had gone off to her room, and was not seen again. This rather shocked Anthony, who felt as though he had always had Miss Rice looking over his shoulder.

Back in the great hall, in front of the fire- place, Beth tried to teach them a card game. Elaine argued over every rule, then ended up winning. Beth was a poor loser and Elaine a poor winner. Beth flounced off to her room.

Diana found sheets and a pajama top of her father's, and fixed a bed for Anthony in the room next to hers.

"Now that that's settled, come on." Elaine pulled at his arm. "I want to show you my secret hide-out."

Down the hall there was a storage room, piled up with boxes and furniture. Elaine had pulled the boxes into a square to make a secret place for herself, lined it with some old blankets, and covered it over with empty cartons.

"Isn't this a good hiding place?" She flopped down, patting the blanket beside her as an invitation to Anthony to join her. "This is where I come when I just can't stand it any longer."

"Can't stand what?"

"Oh, Beth and Diana and -- oh, everybody. I told you I often think about running away. Maybe you could give me some ideas."

"Why would you want to run away? I mean, where would you go?"

"Actually, I'd come back here. It's London I want to get away from, and our awful cousins."

"You mean you live with your cousins?"

Elaine pouted. "Yes -- one big happy family, I DON'T think! Reggie is so superior I could just kick him. And Bertie is -- just plain obnoxious. Then there's Uncle Frank, who's all smiles but is really only thinking of himself, and the way he flatters Beth

is sick-making. And Aunt Victoria, who bosses everyone about and never listens -- **nobody** ever listens in
our family. I'd much rather live here, by myself."

Anthony was silent, feeling depressed. He might
as well have stayed at Washburn. Perhaps what he
should have done was try to make it more of a family
there, instead of running away. Bob and Piggy had
given him some ideas -- he could be nicer to Giles and
the other little ones -- maybe he could even make
friends with Ronnie. Then there was Gerry -- he had
said they were friends, but Anthony didn't really
spend much time with him. He could have been helping
Miss Rice, instead of spending so much time plotting
to run away.

But Elaine was complaining again.

"We lived here until five years ago, but we ran
out of money, and when Uncle Frank offered Daddy a
job, he took it. We begged and begged him not to take
us away." Elaine began to cry. "But he wouldn't
listen. I hate him, too. I hate everybody!"

Anthony looked at her in dismay. Tentatively, he
put out a hand and patted her shoulder.

Out in the corridor, they could hear Diana
calling.

"Oh, I suppose we'd better go." Elaine sat up
and dried her eyes hurriedly. "I don't want her to
find us. You won't tell anyone about this place, will
you? Promise?"

"I promise."

"Come on, then."

That night Anthony lay in bed in the earl's pajama top, in a castle, in a room of his own for the first time in his life. But instead of being happy, his mind was in a whirl and his stomach in a knot.

This was what he had always wanted, wasn't it? Dreamed about, and plotted for?

Then why did he feel like crying?

C H A P T E R   10
****

After breakfast the next morning, Elaine and Anthony helped Diana with the dishes again, and then the countess set up her easel in the playroom at the top of the west tower.

Anthony was placed on the window seat, and the girls, sworn to silence, lay on the floor on big, much-worn cushions.

With a deftness that surprised them, the countess roughed out the face and hair, looking pleased with herself.

She studied Anthony's face, lost in thought. Then she looked down at her daughters, and seemed to be studying them, too.

How would an artist see them, Anthony wondered. Diana, now -- she looks nice, but too still, as if a light had gone out. Beth -- too pretty, really. She had a conceited, spoiled look about her. Elaine frowned a lot.

The countess turned her attention back to Anthony and began to work with a smaller brush.

"Why didn't you ever try painting us, mother?" Elaine asked, breaking her vow of silence already.

"Sh!" said Beth.

But their mother answered absent-mindedly. "I did try, long ago, but it didn't work out. Babies are hard to do -- and perhaps I was too close to the subject to do it properly. And of course your father has always been discouraging..." She broke off.

The girls and Anthony tried to be silent, realizing that she was thinking aloud. Perhaps she'd do it some more!

For most of the morning she worked in silence, absorbed; but occasionally, to their delight, she would mutter something under her breath.

"Merry brown eyes. And his mouth has that child's mobility -- difficult."

When the girls grew restless, the countess finally stopped, looking reluctant to quit.

"Please, may we see it?" Elaine asked eagerly.

"No, no." Her mother reacted automatically, then relented slightly. "Perhaps after tomorrow's sitting."

All four young faces brightened.

"But you'll **have** to get more firewood up from the cellar for tonight's fire," she said sternly.

"There isn't any more. I meant to tell you." Diana got up and brushed off her slacks. "Sam must have taken ill before he got it done."

"I saw where he had been cutting, though," Elaine added. "Over by those cedars grandfather planted. We'd just need to have it brought in."

"Isn't there a handcart by the door?" Anthony asked. "We could all go and get it. Come on. Right after lunch."

Elaine and Beth opened their mouths and shut them again, and Diana smiled.

It seemed natural to all help with lunch and then with the dishes, while Beth, surprisingly, told jokes. They were feeling very silly and in high spirits by the time they got the cart and went off in search of the wood.

"Who's Sam?" Anthony asked as they started off.

"He's the caretaker, and has two rooms off the kitchen." Elaine bent to pick up a golden leaf. "But he took ill a couple of weeks ago, and is staying down in the village just now, with his daughter."

"She checks up on the place every now and then, while he isn't here," Diana added. "Although Rothwick is pretty well built, and doesn't seem to have a lot of the problems with pipes and drains and things that so many places seem to have."

"Maybe we should go and see Sam some time this week," Elaine said. "I like him."

"All right! Good idea! We should have thought of that before," the other girls chimed in.

Anthony looked back at the castle, and pointed. "Is that the Rothwick coat of arms on the back wall? Isn't it on the front, too?"

"That's right." Diana smiled. "I don't know if you can see that rose at the top, from here, but family legend has it that during the War of the Roses, they had the rose on the north side painted white, for

York, and the rose on the south side painted red, for Lancaster, just to keep on good terms with everybody."

"But surely your family was Yorkist?"

"Oh yes, in fact two of our ancestors lost their lives fighting for Richard the Third at Bosworth Field. Thirty men left the castle for Bosworth, and not one of them came back."

Anthony felt his scalp prickle.

"It must have been awful!" Beth shuddered. "All those poor wives and mothers, waiting and waiting."

"Melodrama," Elaine muttered under her breath.

"The earl that got killed was a great friend of Edward IV, and he stayed here several times, the whole court. The knights camped out in this field."

"Did Richard ever come?"

"With Edward, while Edward was king, yes."

Anthony stared around him, picturing the land and castle as it was 500 years ago, seeing it through Richard III's eyes. A thrill of pleasure massaged his backbone, and he couldn't help smiling.

"We lost a lot of history at Bosworth," Beth put in. "There was only a new young countess and a baby son, and they didn't know anything, so now nobody knows. We tried to attract tourists here for a while, but when there's no history, they aren't as interested."

"We lost the secret of the hidden room, too," Elaine added.

They had arrived at the place where Sam had been cutting, and Anthony stopped the cart next to where the cut logs lay, some piled neatly, others lying scattered about. "What secret room?"

"Oh, there's a story that there is one. Father pooh-poohs the whole thing, says it's just a silly old wives' tale. He says almost every castle has a legend about a secret passage -- but most of the time it's rubbish." Diana brushed the hair out of her eyes and went to get another log.

"Well, I believe it," Elaine threw in an armload of smaller sticks.

"You'd believe anything." Beth struggled to get a log tipped into the cart and then stopped to unzip her jacket. "Whew, this is hard work!"

"How would you know whether it's hard or not, since you never do any work, full stop?" scoffed Elaine.

"Neither do you!"

"I've done more than you, Lady Featherbrain."

Beth threw down the log she had just picked up. "Why should I work if I'm not appreciated?"

"Why should WE do it all? You think you're special?"

"Wait a minute, what IS this?" Anthony spread his arms out between the two girls, like a referee at a boxing match. "I ran away from the Home because of all the bickering and quarreling. I thought that in a family, people would care about each other, and be kind to each other. If you keep this up, I'll be running away from here to go back to the Home!"

Beth grinned at him sheepishly. "All right, let's not fight."

Elaine was still scowling.

"Come on, shake hands."

Elaine reluctantly put her hand out, and they went back to loading the cart.

Anthony started them singing again, and Elaine's frown gradually disappeared.

The cart full, they started back to the castle. "Do you suppose we'll ever be able to move back here?" Elaine asked, looking around at the moors.

Diana sighed. "I hope so."

"I hate it in London."

"Me, too." Diana and Elaine looked at each other.

"I didn't think you minded it that much."

Diana shook her head.

"I like it in London," Beth said.

"You would!" Elaine retorted, but subsided after a sharp look from Anthony.

"Didn't you say you had tried opening the castle to tourists? Why didn't you keep it up?" Anthony retrieved a fallen log and they started pulling the cart again.

Diana sighed. "There's just nothing special about dear old Rothwick, except to us, and it's miles from anywhere. We couldn't make a go of it, and Daddy had to borrow some money from Uncle Frank, which is why he can't get out of working for him."

Elaine looked shocked. "I never knew that! Poor Daddy! Then, you mean -- maybe he doesn't really like living in London, either?"

"Of course he doesn't. Does he seem happy to you?"

"Then perhaps -- no wonder he gets mad at the way I carry on about hating it."

"What's everybody got against London? It's exciting!"

"Uncle Frank takes you everywhere because you have a pretty face," Elaine said nastily. "Too bad it's made you so unbearably conceited."

"Since you DON't have a pretty face, I wonder what's your excuse?"

"You two shook hands about ten minutes ago and agreed not to fight," Anthony put in mildly.

"How could anyone put up with her!" Beth stormed.

"You've just got into the habit of quarreling," Anthony said. "You don't HAVE to. Come on, let's get this wood unloaded."

They unloaded in silence, stacking the wood in the cellar. When they were finished, Beth stalked off to her room to read.

"You know, we haven't given Anthony the grand tour of the castle yet," Elaine said to Diana.

"You two go ahead. I think I'll read for a while, too."

"Oh come on, Diana, you're the one who knows the most."

"Well, all right. Ladies and gentlemen, you are now in the Great Hall of Rothwick Castle, built in 1471."

"We don't have much furniture left, just the really antique-y things," Elaine added. "Daddy sold all the comfortable stuff, but he says this belongs to Rothwick, so it stays."

"I like it," said Anthony.

"Mostly 16th century carved oak," Diana said. "We get antique dealers coming sometimes, just to look at it."

"And sometimes Daddy does appraisals on antiques. He really knows a lot about them."

They moved on to the panelled library, with its shelves lined with volumes bound in soft old leather.

"The books are mostly outdated things about farming and so on. Daddy only kept them because they make the library look good." Diana moved on to the grand piano, opened it, and played a few notes idly.

"Can you play the piano?" Anthony asked eagerly, moving over to also touch some notes. It sounded nice.

"No..."

"Come on, this is the only interesting part," Elaine called, and they followed her into the chapel. "Remember about the secret room?" She pointed to some words carved at the top of a pillar. "That's supposed to be where the Bosworth earl left a clue about how to find it, in case he and his son didn't come back."

"They only think that because it makes no sense," Diana said scornfully.

Anthony peered up. "'Way of the cross, tears of -- tross?' What's that? And -- 'Norman dross.' What does all that mean?"

"Nobody knows. The secret died at Bosworth

Field. If the earl really did leave that message, it was too hard for anybody to figure out."

Anthony stared up at the words, hoping for enlightenment. "At least he fought on Richard's side."

"Don't tell me you're a fan of Richard's!" Diana said. "Most people think of him as the Wicked Uncle."

"We have the most awful arguments with Reggie and Bert, our Awful Cousins. They WON'T believe Richard was a good king." Elaine frowned fiercely.

"Yes, it's nice to meet someone who's on our side. Father belongs to the Friends of Richard III." Diana smiled at Anthony.

"But the riddle -- of course you've tried to solve it?"

"Of course. Everyone's had a go, for nearly 500 years. There used to be some 'way of the cross' panels in here, but one of the ancestors had them all taken out, trying to find the secret. He never did, though. You can see the masons' marks where they used to be."

Anthony stepped closer to have a look at the unfamiliar marks.

"When we had tours, there were actually some people who took out penknives and started trying to dig into the walls."

"Yes, Daddy decided it had been a mistake to mention it." Diana sighed. "It was bad planning, really. Daddy paid a huge sum to some man from London to come up and do a fancy booklet, with photographs. We still have boxes and boxes of them. Then he paid for advertising because we started too late to get into the Tourist Office brochures.   And we hired people from the village to be guides. Then when it was a big flop, that was when Daddy had to borrow money to pay everyone off."

Anthony was thinking. "But you're older now -- if you tried again, YOU could be the guides, couldn't you? And now that you know about the Tourist Office, you needn't pay for advertising -- and you already have the booklets..."

The girls looked at him thoughtfully.

"So any income would be profit," said Diana.

"And you could serve teas," Anthony added, looking at Diana. "Lots of castles do. It even sounds to me as if there's plenty of history, if it's presented right. I mean, why pooh-pooh a legend about secret rooms? People like it, even when they know it's just a legend. And the thirty men going off to Bosworth Field?"

"I know," Elaine broke in.   "We could do that play about Bosworth that you wrote last year, Diana. That would add interest, wouldn't it?"

Diana laughed uncertainly. "I don't know..."

"What play is that?"

"We had to write something for history at school, so I did a play -- it's only one act -- about the earl going off to meet Richard. Father liked it, so the five of us acted it out. Reggie was the earl, of course."

"Of course." Elaine giggled. "And a more pompous earl you never saw. Oh dear, they really are awful, Anthony.   They're both fat, and stupid, and snobbish, and selfish, and mean, and -- awful!"

Anthony couldn't help thinking of Ronnie, but decided not to mention him. He felt a strange feeling of loyalty towards Washburn boys, now that he was away from there.

Diana sat down in one of the pews. "It really is awful, Anthony. I'd rather live in your orphan's home."

"No, you wouldn't. It's all boys."

"Really? But isn't it fun? I mean... what IS it like?"

"I suppose it's not so bad. There were some good times." Anthony surprised himself, defending it like that.

"Sounds better than Melby Place. ANYTHING sounds better than Melby Place. I don't know how Beth stands it."

"Do you suppose Mother likes it?"

"Who knows?" Diana sighed. "They don't really tell us much, do they!" She sighed again. "You know how Aunt Victoria says father never laughs and mother never cries? It's almost as if they aren't really alive any more, don't have any feelings. But I can remember father laughing, before the accident that killed Uncle Tony. I was only litte then, but I remember."

Diana's mention of the accident was like suddenly stepping into a cold shower for Anthony. The bare fact in the book hadn't meant much to him, but now...

"Father used to play with me, and laugh, and mother was always singing." Her face had a hurt look, and her mouth twisted briefly. "Then the accident happened, and father was in the hospital for weeks and weeks, and came back with that big scar on his face, and his limp, and he was always cross. Then you were born, Elaine, and mother just left us with Nanny and took up painting, and everything changed. Nanny was nice, but it wasn't the same." She put her head in her arms, leaning against the pew. Was she crying? Anthony couldn't tell. It sounded rather like it.

Anthony laid a sympathetic hand on her shoulder. That accident had changed a lot of people's lives. He felt uncomfortable and guilty, somehow. He wished Diana wouldn't cry.

Elaine came over, too, to pat Diana awkwardly, and after a minute she stopped crying and sat up, drying her eyes. "I'd better go. It must be time to start tea."

"We'll help, won't we, Anthony?"

"If you want to." Diana managed a smile, and they trooped out to the kitchen.

C H A P T E R   11
****

After tea, with the fire snapping merrily in the fireplace (and more appreciated than usual, Beth had said, thinking of all the work they had done), the four of them played Cluedo, while the countess again disapppeared to her room.

Once or twice Elaine started to growl at Beth, but Anthony had learned to see it coming on her face, and managed to turn the conversation to other things.

Diana won the game, deducing that it was the professor who had done it, in the ballroom with a rope.

"I was miles off," Anthony confessed as they put the game away.

"I never win this stupid game," Beth said crossly, stomping off to her room.

Diana stood up and stretched. "Who's for hot chocolate?"

"Us!"

They trailed out to the cold kitchen.

"I'll get out the biscuits," Elaine volunteered.

She got out the tin and then stood staring at the Victorian family scene on the lid.

"What's the matter -- mold?"

"No -- I was just thinking. I think I'll go and get Mother and Beth to join us."

Diana looked at her in surprise. "All right -- good idea!"

Anthony kept an eye on the pan of milk while Diana got out the mugs.

"I guess your mother..."

"What?"

"...isn't the kind who -- who kisses you good-night?"

"No." Flatly.

There was a silence. Then, "Do you do all the cooking at your uncle's?"

"Oh, no. But I like to cook, and Mother doesn't. In fact, it's just lately, when I've said I'd keep house, that Daddy has let us stay up here without him. He said if it was up to Mother to look after us, we'd all starve to death. So now I gladly cook, so we can come up more often and stay longer."

"But you end up doing the washing up, too?"

"Usually. It's nice to have help, though. VERY nice."

Anthony shook his head in wonder. "How can you and Beth be so different?"

"She can't help her good looks. Uncle Frank spoils her -- she'll outgrow it."

"Who'll outgrow what?" Beth walked in and helped herself to a biscuit.

Diana turned away, silent.

"I was being unkind, and Diana was sticking up for you. She thinks you'll have sense enough to outgrow being conceited."

"Oh." Beth turned pink and started to choke on her biscuit. Diana got her a glass of water, and there was an awkward silence for a minute until Elaine came in.

"Mother won't come. She's reading. Haven't we got any more chocolate biscuits?"

Diana poured the hot chocolate into four mugs, and put the fifth one back.

On an impulse, Anthony reached up and got the mug out again. "Couldn't we take some up to her?"

The three sisters looked at each other.

"Why not?" Diana poured the cocoa, and they filed upstairs to their mother's room.

"Who is it?"

Diana didn't answer, but motioned Elaine to open the door. They marched in.

The countess, lying on the bed with a book, looked startled, then pleased.

"You brought me -- but how nice!" She accepted the cocoa gratefully. "I was sorry after I'd told Elaine no. I say no too unthinkingly, I'm afraid." She studied Anthony's face again as she took a sip. "Mm. Nice and warm. It's gotten cold, hasn't it!"

"Would you like a fire?" Diana moved quietly to light it, as Beth and Elaine found places to sit on the bed. Anthony sat at the small and elegant Lady Davenport desk, which he studied curiously.

They sipped their hot chocolate, a little self-consciously. Then Diana tightened her hands around the warm mug.

"Mother, we were talking earlier about whether any of us liked living at Uncle Frank's. Do you?"

"Oh -- London is fascinating. So many art galleries and museums..."

"Mother -- the truth. Please!"

"We must adjust to our circumstances, dear. Victoria and Frank have been very kind."

"Wouldn't you rather live at Rothwick again?"

"I wouldn't!" Beth gave a little bounce that almost spilled everyone's cocoa. Then she felt everyone's accusing eyes on her, and subsided, looking uncertain.

The countess looked at her daughters, and Anthony followed her gaze. They all three look unhappy, he thought. Even Beth, who thinks she IS happy.

The countess rubbed her forehead and sighed. "Everything changed, after the accident," she murmured.

Everyone was silent. Even Diana, who had found strength enough from Anthony to invade her mother's private domain, now could think of nothing to say. Her mother wasn't going to answer the question, that much was obvious. But then, she didn't have to. The answer was in her face.

Anthony, remembering the success of "Ilka Moor," started to sing "All Through the Night," and one by one the other four joined in, the countess singing in harmony.

"Sleep, my child, and peace attend thee,
All through the night..."

They went on happily to "Annie Laurie" and
"Swanee River." Diana took heart from the singing and
went ahead with an idea she had gotten from Anthony
earlier.

She got up, leaned over, and kissed her mother's
cheek. "Good night, Mother."

Elaine followed suit. Beth hesitated, and Diana
gave Anthony a little push. He gave the countess's
cheek a quick peck, and then Beth, not to be outdone,
came forwad with a kiss, too. They all trooped out
smiling.

C H A P T E R   12
****

Next morning, even Beth helped with the dishes, a little.

The countess set up her easel for another painting session. This time she allowed them to look at the results, and was pleased with their delight. It really was going well. But she also had the tournament picture to finish, the one Anthony had interrupted, so after lunch she took her easel up the hill.

"What'll we do?" Elaine flopped down on the rug in front of the fireplace.

"Your mother wanted me to write to the Home..."

"Don't bother, she's forgotten."

Anthony felt relief, but also guilt. If she insisted, perhaps he could just put a blank piece of paper in the envelope. He sighed.

"What about Sam? Weren't we going to visit him?"

"I know, first we ought to make him some get-well cards," Beth said.

"Perhaps I could make him some little cakes, too," Diana added.

Anthony jumped up. "Would you show me how? We were never allowed in the kitchen at the Home."

Diana laughed. "Why don't we all do it? It's about time someone else knew how to do something in the kitchen. And baking is fun."

Beth pouted. "Not me. I'm going to finish my book."

"You won't get any, then," Diana warned.

"What if I lend you my felt-tip markers when we're making cards? The kitchen is just not my place."

Elaine turned on her. "No, your place is a sty, Miss Piggy."

"Wait a minute," Anthony broke in hastily. "What do you mean, Beth, it's not your place?"

"I only meant it's not my thing! I'm all thumbs in the kitchen -- you should see me at school! I didn't mean I was too proud, for goodness sake. You always think the worst of me!"

"Oh well, let it go," Diana said. "How about it, Elaine? Maybe where kitchens are concerned she takes after Mother."

"We'll come," Anthony answered for them both. "See you later, Beth."

Elaine scowled, but she went with Diana and Anthony to the kitchen, and soon seemed to be enjoying herself. Diana made one batch of cakes for Sam, and Elaine and Anthony, copying everything Diana did, made a second batch for the family.

When it was in the oven, they went back to the

Hall, where Beth had gotten out some paper and markers for them, and had begun making a get-well card.

"That's rather nice, Beth." Diana got down on the floor beside her sister. "You must have mother's talent."

Beth looked pleased. "Come on. Let's each make one."

Elaine and Anthony joined them on the floor.

"Do any of you play the piano? I've always wanted to learn," Anthony said.

"No, none of us do, though I'd like to learn, too." Diana started drawing a rose. "I asked about it, in London, but of course there's no piano at Melby Place."

"Daddy used to play, didn't he?"

"That's right." Diana sat back to look critically at her work. "But he hasn't for ages. We ought to ask him to when he comes up."

The countess came silently in, looked with surprise at their work, and then began building a fire in the fireplace.

Beth looked up. "It IS getting cold, isn't it! I wish it was summer again, and we could go over to the bay and go swimming."

"I wouldn't mind going to a tropical island for a swim, some day," Diana said. "The bay is awfully cold, if you ask me."

"Remember that program where people tell what books they'd take to a desert island?" Anthony asked. "I was wondering the other day what kind of **people** I'd like to take. What about you?"

"Someone who knew a lot of jokes," said Elaine.

"Someone who'd laugh at mine!" countered Beth.

"Someone who really listened to you when you talked," Diana added, and Anthony saw her mother wince.

"Someone who can cook --"

"NOT someone who got cross all the time..."

"If you mean me...!"

"Someone considerate..."

"And nice -- you know --"

"Anyone except Reggie and Bert!"

"Amen!"

The girls laughed, and Anthony, too. "There's a boy called Ronnie at the Home who sounds a bit like your cousins, but somehow, now that I'm not there, I can actually think of one or two times when he's been all right."

"Oh, I suppose Reggie and Bert must have some good points, somewhere." Diana made a face as she said it.

"Traitor!" Elaine said, but smiled.

Beth sat back on her heels. "It's too bad, isn't it, that the five of us live together at Melby Place and none of us are friends? The only friend I've got is at school."

"Me, too," said Elaine, "Except Anthony."

Anthony threw down his marker. "For heaven's sake, can't you three be friends?"

The three looked at each other uncomfortably, and the sudden silence made the countess look up from her book. She sniffed.

"Is something cooking?"

"The cakes!" They all leaped up to go and check.

Then of course they had to sample them, and have a glass of milk. They finished the get-well cards they had started, and by that time it was raining...

"We'll go tomorrow," Diana suggested as she started peeling potatoes for tea.

That evening, after the dishes had been done, they lay in a row on the rug in front of the fire.

The countess, for once, came and sat down with them, without even a book.

"What's that you're doing, Mother?" Beth asked.

"I decided to crochet some slippers for a Christmas present. There's plenty of wool -- would anyone else like to make something?"

"Oh, I would!" Diana jumped up. "Would you teach me?"

Elaine turned to Anthony. "Housewife stuff," she scoffed. "I'M not going to sit at home and crochet when I grow up, I'm going to get a job and see the world."

Diana sighed and rolled her eyes. "No question who's the thorn in THIS rose garden."

Elaine sniffed. "Well, it's the family tradition, isn't it?"

Anthony rolled over to look at her. "Another tradition? Tell me about it!"

Elaine shrugged. "It's pretty vague, only that the family holds a thorn with the rose. Something to do with the War of the Roses, we suppose. Originally it was called 'Richard's thorn.'"

"Richard the Third's?"

"Could be -- or it could be anybody."

Anthony lay on his back and looked up at the high plastered ceiling with its decorations of roses and coats of arms. "I don't know a whole lot about Richard, actually. What really did happen with the nephews, does anyone know?"

"No, I don't think anyone does." Diana looked up from her work. "They only know that the nephews disappeared, and that no one seemed to have a satisfactory explanation of where they went..."

"So that later on, when Henry Tudor came along, all he had to do was tell everyone that Richard had killed them off, and there was no one that could prove otherwise." Beth twirled her hair around her finger. "But Richard didn't NEED to kill them off, that's the big difference. And since Tudor killed off practically everyone that had the remotest claim to the throne, but Richard had been pretty lenient for those days, it makes more sense to suppose that Tudor killed the nephews."

"But there must have been some people who knew the real story?"

"Perhaps -- but Tudor was pretty good at suppressing the evidence." Diana took up the story. "Did you know that it's been proven that King Edward had been betrothed to another lady before he married Elizabeth Woodville? And that was enough, in those days, to make the marriage invalid. So Parliament declared Richard to be the true and rightful king. He wasn't a usurper, at all.

"Then, after Richard's death, Tudor ordered all the evidence about that destroyed, so that when he married Edward's daughter, she was legitimate again, and his claim to the throne was strengthened. He had one of his own flunkies write a history, and that's what people have copied all these years, not the true story. Even Shakespeare fell for it, and popularized it. Of course, it was still the Tudor dynasty in his day."

"Poor old Richard." Beth sighed. "His son died, and then his wife, and a lot of his friends deserted him, especially at Bosworth -- he must have had a sad life at the end."

"It was a time of treachery, wasn't it." Diana bent over her crocheting. "I mean, people don't lie and cheat and betray nowadays, do they?"

"Uncle Frank does it all the time," Elaine said.

"Elaine!" Beth was shocked.

"Well, isn't he always bragging about the tricks he pulls off in business?"

"But that's **business**..." Beth's voice trailed off.

"I think perhaps you've put it a bit strongly, Elaine," said her mother calmly.

"Well --" Elaine made an obvious struggle to be reasonable. "I suppose I did."

The countess laid down her crocheting and stood up. "Why don't I make the hot chocolate tonight?"

Diana looked at her in surprise. "That would be nice!" she said gratefully.

Once again, Anthony saw her mother wince, as she left for the kitchen.

CHAPTER 13
****

Thursday morning came half-awake in a misty dawn which soon darkened into a howling storm that, even indoors, had a dampening effect on everyone.

"The light's not right for a portrait session this morning," the countess said, and returned to bed with another book.

Diana tried to light a fire in the fireplace, but the wind came blowing down the chimney, filling the room with smoke. Diana hastily put it out again. "These old chimneys just go straight up," she said with disgust.

"Yes, when the smoke is cleared, Anthony, you should get inside and look up. You can see daylight." Elaine flapped at the smoke with a kitchen towel.

"Not today he won't see daylight. Look at how black the sky is!" Beth had taken refuge by the big windows that looked out to the east.

"Oh, pull the draperies, and let's have some more toast to warm us up."

"Can't. We're all out of bread." Diana wiped

her eyes, which were watery from the smoke. "But we do need to clear the smoke out of here."

"Why don't we just clear ourselves out? It'll go eventually. Let's go up in the playroom."

They trooped up the stairs to the west tower, where the painting sessions had been, Anthony thinking guiltily that it was because he was there that they had run out of bread. Perhaps he should offer them his five pounds -- no, they wouldn't take it -- they'd feel insulted. What was the good of having money, then? He puzzled over it as they climbed the stairs.

Even in the playroom, nothing went right. Elaine was moody and couldn't decide on anything she wanted to do. Beth found she'd developed a pimple, and retired from view.

Diana crossly put on her mack to go out in the storm and put up the flag that was a signal for the bakery van to include them in his rounds.

Anthony's feelings were in a turmoil again. Last night had been so nice -- the countess had taken the hint and kissed them all good night, and Anthony had started to have high hopes about this family getting together.

And now look at them, all off in their own corners again, snapping at each other. He despaired of them!

But by noon the storm had relented somewhat, the bread had arrived, and Anthony's optimism returned with the smell of lunch.

"I'm still curious about that inscription in the

chapel," he said as Diana ladled out the soup. "You never said whether 'tross' means anything."

Beth shrugged. "We're all bored with that old stuff."

"You sound like Reggie," Elaine snapped. "Anyway, speak for yourself. I'm not bored with it."

"We don't know that tross means anything -- it isn't in our dictionary." The countess sighed. "The closest anyone seems to have come is the French word, 'trousse,' which means a bundle or a case -- and the word 'trousseau' can mean a bunch of keys, so of course the family has tended to think in that direction. But if ever there was a bunch of keys, it's been long gone."

Beth was still feeling belligerent. "I shouldn't think anyone would want to find the secret, anyway, considering the curse."

"That's a lot of old superstition!"

But Anthony was interested. "Come on, tell me about the curse."

Elaine and Beth fell silent, glancing at their mother.

"I suppose most castles have their skeletons in the cupboard," she obliged him by saying. "One of ours is the story, probably untrue, that the man who built this castle, back in the 15th century, was killed when it was finished, in order to preserve the secret of the hidden room. The legend is that as he died, he placed a curse on the family.

"I think myself that the story was probably invented to explain the misfortune at Bosworth, when the

Earl and his son, and 30 villagers besides, were killed, leaving only women and children here." She buttered a slice of bread.

"Of course we don't believe in curses, but although accidents happen in every family, in THIS family they get blamed on the curse."

Anthony glanced around at the somber faces, knowing that they were all thinking of the accident that had killed their Uncle Tony.

"It's best not to mention this in front of my husband," the countess went on. "Anyway, the horrible part isn't the curse, is it, but the thought that someone might kill just to preserve a secret."

"But they WERE cruel in those days." Diana shuddered.

"Probably the secret room is guarded by workmen's bones," Elaine said with relish.

"All the more reason for not finding it, then," Beth retorted.

"The people in the village all lost husbands and sons, too," Diana said slowly. "Isn't it strange that in spite of that, they've stayed loyal, all these centuries -- and even now, all we have to do is send up a flare, and they come running to see if we need help."

"We haven't shown Anthony the flare gun yet." Beth suddenly looked less moody.

"Yes, Bloody Beth knows all..."

"Elaine!"

"...about guns and shooting. Uncle Frank has made her an expert at shooting baby rabbits."

Beth's pretty face turned red. "You know very well I only shot one -- and I felt so awful about it, I've never shot at anything but targets since!" She burst into tears.

"Oh, Beth, I'm sorry!" Elaine stumbled over the unaccustomed words. "I didn't know that you -- that you'd felt awful. I--I'm sorry, honestly. Why didn't you ever tell us?"

Beth dried her eyes and looked at her younger sister in surprise. "I suppose I never thought you'd be sympathetic, you were all being so beastly to me..."

"I'm sorry, too, Beth," Diana added, and the three smiled at each other shyly.

"Uncle Frank HAS taught Beth a lot, though," Elaine said more kindly. "Maybe it's time we all learned how to fire the flare."

She turned to Anthony. "It's in case there's any trouble up here. We fire it off, and the police constable comes roaring up with whoever else happens to be around. It started a long time ago, before the village had telephones, and then when we DID get a telephone in, the lines kept going down anyway, so the custom stayed on. And now the phone is disconnected for the winter, so -- not that we ever use it except at Guy Fawkes, and then only for fun!"

"On the contrary, I understand Sam used it when he took ill," the countess said. "In which case, perhaps it ought to be looked at, cleaned and so on.."

It wasn't where it should have been, on a shelf in the kitchen, but they found it in Sam's room. Beth

showed them how to clean it and load it, explaining
that it worked on the same general principle as the
rifles their uncle kept.

"Look, the rain has stopped. We should go and
see Sam."

"Yes, we'd better, while there are still some
cakes left!"

"Wait for me, I'm going to change." Beth started
for the door.

"Whatever for?" Elaine looked down at her own
jeans and jumper.

"It's all right for YOU to go visiting looking
like a tramp, you're still a child..."

Elaine made a face. "Oh, no! If you're going to
go as Lady Bountiful, I think I'm going to throw up!"

Beth turned pink again. "Diana! You're going
to change, aren't you?"

Diana looked down at her woolen slacks and velour
jumper, and then at Beth's tweed skirt and jacket. "I
don't think I will -- it's so cold out there -- muddy,
too, probably. We hardly need to change, anyway, just
to drop in on someone..."

"Oh well, if you're going to be peasants!" Beth
flounced toward the door. "Come on, then."

They filed out into the gray afternoon and
started down the gravelled drive. The rain was holding off, but just barely. In the forest, most of the
trees were now looking more like winter, with only a
rare leaf still clinging.

There was very little in the village -- a cluster
of cottages with their backs to the fields which

supplied them with a living; a small shop in the front room of someone's house; a telephone kiosk.

Someone now lived in the small schoolhouse where all three girls had learned to read and write; the few children in the village were now bussed 15 miles away to a larger school. That there was a police constable in the village was mostly because the castle was there and progress had not changed tradition that much.

They stopped at a small stone cottage with roses climbing around the door, and asked to speak to Sam.

Both the caretaker and his daughter, Rose, were pink with pleasure at the unexpected visit, and beamed to think the girls had made get-well cards and even some cakes, for him.

Of course they must have a cup of tea, and Rose went to the kitchen to put the kettle on.

Sam, lying on the davenport by the fire, shook his head. "Seeing you from this angle makes me realize how grown up you're all becoming. You'll be getting married before we know it."

The girls smiled.

"Nearly sixteen, aren't you, Lady Diana? You'll be snapped up first, a beauty like you."

Diana and Beth exchanged glances of surprise. "Me! It's Beth that's the beauty."

But Sam was shaking his head. "Oh, you're all pretty lasses, right enough, but it's you, my lady -- you look just like your grandmother, who was greatly renowned for her beauty. Greatly renowned."

Elaine gave Beth a sly nudge, and Beth pouted.

"Tell us about her," Elaine said sweetly.

"There's much to tell." Sam settled himself back on the pillows. "Much to tell. She was a beauty all right, but, if you'll pardon my saying so, it turned her head. She would come here for parties at Rothwick and be downright cruel to the earl, your grandfather. Of course he was in love with her -- half the young men in Yorkshire were. Oh, we held our breaths, here in Nether Rothwick, waiting for her to make her choice. We were hoping for his lordship, of course, because that's what he wanted -- but oh, we thought, that one will be a handful if he ever gets her!

"The field seemed to narrow down to three. There was the Earl of Medburgh, who took his title from lands in Scotland but was never there. He had settled in Scarborough because he liked the sailing -- a snobbish man who spent his money foolishly but seemed to have plenty of it. He was a bit older nor the other two, and some of us thought he probably would be able to handle her better -- but he might break her spirit, too; people didn't trust him much. There were tales of things he had done in Scotland that were -- but never mind.

"Then there was Viscount Scarsdale, the handsomest young man you were ever likely to see, and he had plenty of money, too, but empty in the head -- no substance to him. Yet her ladyship seemed to like his company the best. He was fun-loving and young, and with her looks and his, everyone turned their heads to look at them, perhaps that was why.

"While those two were flattering her up and turning her head still more, our Lord Rothwick was trying to court her, too. He was good-looking enough, though he hadn't the looks of the Viscount; nor did he have enough money to compete with Lord Medburgh. Still, she deigned to give him some of her attention.

"Then came the Christmas ball at Scarsdale, and her ladyship was Lord Scarsdale's partner for the evening. Lord Medburgh went alone, hoping to be able to take up some of her time.

"But your grandfather decided on a different course. He went down to London and went to see Marie-Louise Delacroix, a celebrated actress of that day. He got an introduction from a mutual friend, explained his problem, and begged her to come with him to the ball. She, so they say, laughed and thought it would be a good joke, so she came.

"You should have seen the eyes popping out when she walked in on his lordship's arm! Next to her -- mind you, she was an actress, so she well knew how to enhance her looks, and how to charm a man, besides -- next to her, your grandmother looked and acted like a spoiled child, which of course she was, begging your pardon.

"Miss Delacroix had Lord Scarsdale panting after her in no time, and then she set out to charm Lord Medburgh. Of course he was flattered -- and at about that time, your grandmother flew into a temper tantrum and started insulting Miss Delacroix.

"Whereupon your grandfather removed her bodily from the hall, gave her a spanking over his knee out in the foyer, and took her home."

Sam crowed with laughter. "You can imagine the talk in the countryside! For a few months, your grandmother wouldn't see any of them, she was so angry and so mortified. Scarsdale and Medburgh faded out of the picture. But your grandfather kept on sending flowers, month after month, until finally she grew up a little, realized that here was someone who was genuine, with some depth to him -- and who really loved her for herself. So she finally relented. Their wedding was one of the high points of the year, in York Minster -- and much to everyone's surprise, they got along very happily together.

"But here, I've been talking too long. Here's Rose with the tea. Have some chocolate biscuits!"

Later, as they started walking home in the cold wind, Beth seemed silent and thoughtful.

"Come on," Diana said, "let's stop at the shop. We'll need extra things for the weekend, with Daddy coming."

A gloom seemed to settle on Anthony. Not only was the father going to appear -- and it seemed unlikely he would be friendly -- but he was also beginning to realize that he was costing them money, and if they really didn't have much -- oh, he should never have come! But -- he shrugged -- he was here, so he might as well make the best of the last two days.

They turned into the shop. It was a bit dim inside, and crowded once the four of them had squeezed in, so it was a moment before they realized that a tall young man was leaning against the counter, looking at them with an unfriendly expression on his tanned face.

"Why -- Rob! How nice to see you!" Diana sounded rather breathless.

Rob nodded stiffly and said nothing.

"Are -- are you still at school?" Diana faltered.

"College. Naval architecture."

"Oh! How nice for you -- you've always loved boats..." She faltered again, dropping her eyes before his rather fierce gaze.

"Rob used to come sailing with us when we were growing up," Beth explained to Anthony.

"Yes, until your father decided a policeman's son wasn't good enough to be with his precious daughters," Rob broke in bitterly.

Diana drew in her breath sharply, and turned pale. "Oh, Rob, that's not true!"

Rob pushed himself upright, standing taut as a bow. "He as much as said so, didn't he?"

"But he -- he was so upset those days, when the tourist business wasn't working out..."

"And I suppose that earls..." the emphasis was contemptuous and harsh, "...can hurt other people whenever they please, unlike us ordinary mortals!" He turned abruptly and strode out of the shop.

There was a moment's unhappy silence, and then the shopkeeper's voice boomed out. "Now then, ladies -- and gentleman -- what can I do for you today?"

Diana, still pale, fumbled in her pocket for her list, and silently handed it over. Anthony realized

he was clenching his hands together, and forced himself to relax. If a policeman's son wasn't good
enough, where would an orphan boy come in the queue?

"Let's get out of here," Elaine muttered at his
elbow, and they squeezed out.

"Daddy WAS awful to Rob," she said as they
started walking slowly up the road. "Diana wasn't
there when it happened. I don't blame him for being
angry, but I wish he wouldn't take it out on Diana --
she really likes him, I think."

"What happened, anyway?"

Elaine looked puzzled. "We were friends with
everyone at school here in the village, in the old
days. We almost always took Rob and his brother John
with us when we went sailing at Scarborough. That was
when we still had our catboat and the dinghy. But
when the money was running out, and it looked as if
we'd have to move to London..." She paused, looking
regretful. "I can see, now, that of course Daddy
didn't want to go -- anyway, Daddy was horrid about
selling the boat -- we all of us were begging him not
to -- we didn't understand what it was all about. He
was horrid to Rob, too, just because he took our side
and asked him not to sell it. Rob wouldn't come near
us after that. Diana even wrote him a letter, but it
was returned unopened.

"But look, isn't that Rob down there by the
brook?" Elaine looked uncertainly at Anthony. "Do
you think..." She stopped.

"...We ought to try and talk to him? Why not?
It couldn't be much worse, could it?"

Elaine gulped. "Let's go, then." She gripped Anthony's hand tightly as they slid down the bank to the brook.

"Hello, Rob," Elaine said boldly.

He looked up at them. "Oh, it's you." He turned back and tossed another pebble into the brook.

"You don't have to be angry with US, do you?" Elaine said. "I mean, it's not our fault Daddy was horrid, is it?"

"You needn't think you're better than everybody, because you're not," Rob said.

"We don't, honestly. Well, maybe Beth does, but Diana says she'll get over it. Come on, why not come back to the castle with us? Daddy isn't there, even."

"I don't go where I'm not welcome."

Elaine stamped her foot. "But I'm telling you you ARE welcome. Aren't you listening?"

To Anthony's surprise, Rob threw back his head and laughed heartily. "Same old Elaine," he finally said, shaking his head.

"And same old Diana, too, you'll see. Please come?"

"Tell you what, I'll walk you to your door. All right? I'm Rob Bradford," he said to Anthony, holding out his hand.

Anthony shook it. "I'm Anthony -- uh, a friend of Elaine's."

They climbed the bank back up to the road, and there were Beth and Diana, loaded down with shopping bags.

Rob grinned sheepishly at them and held out his hand to Diana. "Peace?"

"Oh, yes, please, peace!" Diana's face lit up.

"I suppose it was my fault if you thought we were snobs," Beth said frankly. "I've been rather a twit about that." Everyone laughed and clapped her on the back, and her face brightened.

"Here, let me have those," Rob said, taking the bags from Diana. "Elaine's talked me into walking you home -- if that's all right."

"Good for Elaine!" Diana smiled, and for the first time Anthony realized how beautiful she really was, when she looked happy.

"Why not stay for tea?"

"Not -- not yet. Maybe someday." Rob looked towards the sea. "Have you still got 'Pegasus?' I haven't seen her..." he asked with a slight frown, as if not wanting to admit he had looked for their boat.

"No, Daddy went ahead and sold it." Diana sighed.

"We went broke and had to move to London, and we hate it," Elaine said in a rush.

"Elaine!" Diana and Beth both turned on her. But Rob looked startled and thoughtful.

"I've just bought a small sailboat," he said after a moment. "I'm just fitting her out. By next summer, I can offer YOU a sail."

The three girls beamed at him.

"Super!" breathed Elaine.

"That would be great!"

"We'd love it!."

Anthony sighed, realizing his visit was almost over. There would be no sailing for him. Only two more days, and then... When he thought about the earl, his heart started beating painfully. The girls didn't seem to be afraid of him, but he was their father. Everyone else seemed to think of him as pretty unpleasant. Sort of like the giant in Jack and the Beanstalk. Out for blood.

At the door of the castle, Rob handed back the groceries and said goodbye a good deal more pleasantly than he had said hello.

"Bundle up tomorrow," he said. "The radio says snow's coming. Can you believe it?"

"Oh no!" Elaine wailed. "It's only October -- I hope it's not true!"

Rob shrugged and started down the hill. They waved until he was out of sight, and then ran inside.

That evening, the countess suggested a Scrabble game, and even gave herself a handicap. It helped take Anthony's mind off the Earl of Rothwick.

"Mother, did you know Grandmother Rothwick?" Beth asked over the hot chocolate.

"Oh yes, indeed."

"Sam was telling us about her courtship. And he says Diana looks like her."

The countess looked over at Diana. "Why, yes, I suppose she does! Of course, I didn't meet her until she was older, but -- yes, there is a resemblance. Perhaps you would dress up in a period ball gown, Diana, and be a model for a portrait of your grandmother. I never understood why there wasn't one, she was such a famous beauty."

"What was she like when you knew her?"

"Mm. Very pleasant and down-to-earth. She and your grandfather seemed to be devoted to each other." There was as touch of wistfulness in her voice. "Even though she came from a wealthy family, she didn't seem to mind living at Rothwick with much less money; in fact, she loved it here. But I never knew her well. She died before we were married."

Beth was silent for a moment, and then finished off her hot chocolate. "I've just made up my mind."

"About time!"

"About what?"

"Oh, stop! About -- I think I **would** rather live here. I hadn't thought about it much, but -- well, our roots are here -- and I'd forgotten how much fun it **could** be, if we were more like a family. And in London they -- well -- they want to buy friendship, don't they. I mean, all those nice things Uncle Frank has done, it's as if then he expects you to do whatever he wants." She hunched her shoulders. "I've heard Uncle Frank telling Aunt Victoria that with my looks I could marry someone rich, and that would solve all our problems. Do you know, I actually **agreed** with that when I heard it? Now I'm beginning to think it's a rather horrid idea. I mean, I'm a person, not a -- a statue to be sold to the highest bidder. And besides, you can't buy happiness, can you!"

There was a moment of astonished silence.

Then Elaine flew over and hugged Beth, and Diana put an arm around her, too.

"This is great! If we're a united front, then maybe we can persuade Daddy that we ought to stay!"

The countess went over to join the hugging. As she put her arms around the girls, she glanced at Anthony, who was struggling between feeling pleased and feeling left out.

"Anthony, you've been so good for us." She held out her hand to him. His face lit up as he joined them. Oh, if only...

C H A P T E R   14
****

Anthony was still thinking "if only" the next
morning, as they resumed the portrait sitting. But he
seemed to get no further than "when the earl comes,"
for his heart to sink.

"Come on, everybody's to do some art work this
morning. I was impressed with those cards you made
for Sam." The countess handed out paper and charcoal.
"Let's see what you can do. It needn't be a person,
if you think that's too hard. You could start on a
part of this room, or the view from the window --
whatever you'd like."

Silence settled on the room as they all worked.
Elaine and then Beth got impatient with themselves and
started over. Diana was doing a sketch of her mother
at the easel. With the less formal atmosphere, all
three stole admiring glances at the portrait as it
progressed.

"Oh," Elaine cried out at one point. "Why can't
mine look like that?"

They all laughed, and then Diana and Beth
exclaimed over their mother's work, too. Anthony

joined them to have a look, and was speechless. Did she really see him like that? He glanced at her shyly.

"What I don't understand," said Diana, peering at it more closely, "is why Daddy is so mean and critical about your work."

"Well, he IS an expert." The countess sighed.

"Didn't you say no-one had seen your work?" asked Anthony? "Even your family?"

"Not for several years, at least."

"Then perhaps he would like it, now?"

The countess hesitated, and then said reluctantly, "I think I'd rather not find out. I paint for my own pleasure, and only for that. If any expert, my husband or anyone, told me it was no good, it would take me a long time to take pleasure in it again. That's why I don't show anyone -- I'm a coward."

Diana's face fell. "I was hoping -- you know -- if you could make some money with it..." Her voice trailed off.

"I'm sorry. I know it's a weak way to feel..."

Anthony tried to reassure her. "It must be hard, being married to an expert. The standards would be so high."

"Yes. Yes, it is hard."

"Does he paint, too?"

"No, but he does appraising sometimes. Of paintings as well as of furniture. I'm sure he'd rather do that full-time, instead of working with my brother-in-law, but somehow he never gets out of debt with Frank. There's always some new favor."

"Oh!" Beth's face was flaming. "Is that why Daddy didn't want me to take gifts from Uncle Frank? I thought he was just being mean! Oh, I'm so stupid!"

The countess wasn't listening. "Perhaps he has some fears of his own, too," she said thoughtfully.

Elaine sniffed. "Seems to me a real artist like you would be a better judge than someone who can't even draw."

"Yes, really, Mother," Beth added. "Not that Daddy isn't a good judge, but you have your own judgement, your own taste, and you should trust that. Didn't you used to tell us that when we were little? Everyone has different tastes, you've always said. So, if Daddy's taste is different, that doesn't mean your work isn't good. You oughtn't to listen to what anyone else says, only go by your own judgement."

"She's right, mother," Diana put in. "So how about it -- what do you honestly think: is your work good?"

Mother and daughter looked at each other for a long, thoughtful moment.

Then the mother took a deep breath. "Yes, it is."

They all smiled at each other.

"We've got to really make plans about living at Rothwick, before Daddy comes," Elaine said later as they sat by the fire, eating lunch.

Diana straightened her back and sighed. "I remember Daddy saying we needed 100 visitors a week in spring and autumn, and 100 a day in summer -- more than that on weekends, to make up for bad days -- in order to manage. We didn't get anywhere near that many."

"But it depends on what your expenses are, and what you charge, and what you offer, doesn't it?" Anthony looked around the room as if trying to judge its worth.

"Some places serve medieval banquets, and take in lodgers," Beth said with a tentative look at Diana. "Could we manage anything like that? I should think tourists would like to stay in a real 15th century castle."

"It would be awfully hard work. But if we all DID work..."

"And if mother doesn't want to exhibit her work, how about different exhibits, with different artists? Aren't they always eager to exhibit? Maybe Anthony could ask Marcus Elliot."

"That's an idea!"

"What about that play of Diana's?" Anthony put in. "Couldn't it be expanded? I don't see why you say there's no history here. There's the secret room, even more intriguing because it's still a mystery. Then there's the builder's curse, and Bosworth, and even your grandmother -- I should think you could make a smashing play about all that -- and about Richard the Third, too, why not? If most people still think of him as the Wicked Uncle, it's about time they learned the other side. And after all, he did come here."

"Yes, why not?"

"Daddy's always been a bit squeamish about the curse and the secret room, but we'll just have to tell him it's our history, too, and we want to make it work for us!"

"Perhaps if we got the play all written, he'd see the tourist value!" Beth's eyes glowed. "We could add some romantic bits -- the young countess and her baby, waiting for her husband's return -- couldn't we take poetic license and do grandmother's romance as if she were the one? Then it could all be in the same century."

"I know who'd play the countess," Elaine began grumpily, but subsided as Diana and Anthony both frowned at her.

"Let's get the play written, then," said Anthony. "That'll be fun! And we'll make sure there's a good part for you, too, Elaine. In fact, how about you being the earl? You'll all have to take men's parts."

"Let's see." Diana got a pad of paper and a pencil and started making notes. "We'll want three acts. First the builder discusses the plans for a secret room with the earl, the earl tells the servant to throw the builder off the tower, and then the builder screams the curse..."

"The second act can be the romantic part -- let's see, we'll need the earl and his two rivals, the lady, and the London actress -- the grand ball, with King Richard there..."

"That's too many of us -- we'll have to get Rob and John in it, too."

"I know just the thing to end the play -- after a servant comes in and tells the countess that no-one is coming back from Bosworth, the ghost of the builder comes on and laughs a horrible laugh!" Elaine grinned ghoulishly.

"We can add a bit about Henry Tudor already telling lies about Richard..."

They went on planning happily, while the countess listened thoughtfully, and the sun warmed the gray stones of the castle.

In London, the sun was not warming anything. It was another damp day, in a damp week.

In his small study, the earl of Rothwick was gazing out the window at the rose garden. He was absently tapping his wife's letter on the palm of his hand as his thoughts wandered bleakly around in circles.

He looked down at the letter once again, his mouth twisting, and then he put it in his pocket, unopened. He found her letters painful, they were so cold and distant. He had a lot of work to get done, in any case, if he was going to make it to Yorkshire by tomorrow evening; this Rundale project was going ahead fast -- too fast for his liking -- but Frank was pleased about it. He fully expected to pass the million mark with this one. Well, more power to him.

His partner and brother-in-law. Rothwick felt his face twist again. Partner! It was Frank's company, from start to finish. Rothwick was only a front man to impress people. 'Meet my partner, the earl...' And he was a glorified bookkeeper. He detested both jobs.

But he was caught in the company, oh so neatly, through his obligations to dear, kind Frank. Frank had known how to play on his false pride, his guilt. Of course Rothwick wanted to pay his share of the living expenses at Melby Place, so that was deducted from his salary. Of course the girls must go to a good private school, as Frank's boys did -- and that was deducted from his salary. And when he finally had managed to save a thousand pounds and offered it to Frank as part payment on the loan, Frank wouldn't take it.

Frank wasn't ever going to let this fish slip away, Rothwick thought with despair. Every favor he does for any of us -- and he does many, though I don't want them -- has strings attached. The message is less than subtle: I owe it to Frank to stay here.

Take this latest business about a horse for Beth. He groaned inwardly. Wasn't Beth old enough to realize how her greedy acceptance of everything from Frank was tying him, trapping him, ever more closely in an impossible situation?

He took a deep breath and rested his forehead on his fists. No, of course she was just a child. He couldn't blame her. But his stomach was twisting into knots again.

He stared down at his desk, feeling a kind of panic. He couldn't even join his family at Rothwick for the holidays -- Frank must be afraid that he might get too re-attached to his old home.

Rothwick stifled a groan just in time, as Victoria walked in without knocking, as she always did.

"Oh, there you are. Still working? Just wanted to remind you that we're going out to dinner with Rundale and Arabella tonight."

"I thought I'd beg off, as a I have a number of..."

"Oh, nonsense. This is to celebrate the final agreement on the project. You MUST come."

"The final agreements aren't until Monday."

"But they can't celebrate that night, don't you remember? Anyway Arabella is like me -- any excuse will do for a party. See you at 7. DON'T be late."

Victoria swept out, and Rothwick wondered anew how two sisters could be so different. But poor Daphne -- anyone might have retreated into a private world after all that had happened. The accident that had made a monster out of him, and -- killed Tony -- he still couldn't think of it without anguish. It had been his fault. HE had killed Tony -- and then to top it off, the worst of it was that he'd benefitted from Tony's death, inherited the title, Rothwick, everything.

He clenched and unclenched his fists, and sighed, feeling the usual depression settle over him. He had rejected everyone. He had even rejected Daphne, turned her away, because he had hated himself so. He had retreated into a shell, doing nothing except feel sorry for himself for years, as the money all dribbled away through lack of his care. Then the half-baked

idea of trying to make Rothwick Castle a tourist spot
-- what a financial disaster that had been. It was
his own fault, again -- he'd been too half-hearted and
too proud. And now, Melby Place!

He could hardly bear living here, but it seemed
the best thing for the rest of the family. Daphne was
always off by herself, anyway, fiddling with her
paints, so it hardly mattered where she lived. And of
course Beth loved all the attention; Diana had always
been quiet; Elaine was at an awkward age.

Poor Tony. Rothwick sighed again. What would
their lives have been like if he had lived? HE'd be
at Rothwick now, with a wife and a family -- and what
would I be doing?

It was a thought he hadn't faced before. Would
he have been the same sour, bitter man, working for
Frank? But he wouldn't have been worth much to Frank,
with no earl's title to offer.

He smiled grimly. At least all this had taught
him a few things -- like the hollowness of a title.
It's almost made a Quaker out of me, he thought. If
I'd known, 12 years ago, I would never have used the
title. Wonder if I could put a stop to it at this
late date? THAT would put a crimp in Frank's style,
all right! He smiled again.

But this wasn't getting the work done. He bent
over his papers.

The play at Rothwick that evening was a decided
success. At least to the players, since there was no

audience. The countess had had to step into a few parts, too.

It had a lot of drama, excitement, and possibilities for great costumes, they all decided over hot chocolate. It also played well in the great hall, against the huge gray stones and Flemish tapestries.

They toasted each other, their faces shining in the orange glow from the fire, and then Beth asked the awkward question. "Will Daddy like it, do you think? Will he let us put it on, for tourists?"

Diana turned to her mother, an appeal in her eyes. "Do you think we can talk Daddy into coming back here to live?"

The countess avoided her eyes and looked down at the floor. "He doesn't listen to me," she said faintly.

"He doesn't listen to us, either," said Elaine. "But Mother, wouldn't he HAVE to listen to you if you put your foot down?"

The countess smiled wryly and shook her head. "I'm not very good at standing up to him, haven't you noticed?"

"Maybe Beth should ask him -- she's everybody's favorite..." Elaine was obviously struggling to keep jealousy out of her voice, but wasn't entirely successful.

"Ho ho." Beth laughed without humor. "It's only Uncle Frank who lets me have my way -- and don't you realize he has selfish reasons for that? As for

Daddy, he treats me like a silly toy. But I'll ask him if you want me to."

"What do you think, Anthony?" Diana turned to him.

"Why don't you all ask him, together? Your mother, too. It won't kill you if he says no at first, will it? You needn't be afraid to ask, and keep on asking -- even insist!"

"Still, I AM afraid -- afraid we'll never move back here." Elaine put her head down on her mother's lap.

"I thought I couldn't stand it at the Home, either," Anthony said slowly, looking at her with sympathy. "But now I think I could go back there and help make it more of a family. Or wherever I'm sent. What I mean is, sure, it's wonderful to have something to hope for and dream about, but you CAN be more of a family, even if you have to stay at Melby Place. If you don't like it there, isn't that all the more reason for you to stick together, and be friends, and help each other put up with it?"

"Anthony's right!" Diana didn't sound like the quiet one now. "We ought to all pledge to stick together, whether we manage to live at Rothwick or not."

"Yes!"

"All right."

"Let's do it!"

They started to join hands in a circle, and Beth and Diana each held out a hand for Anthony to join them.

"Come on, Anthony, you're in this, too. One for all and all for one!"

They all glowed at each other. Anthony had to swallow hard, and his chest hurt a little. But this was more like it!

The goodnight kisses seemed firmly established. The countess said she'd wash up the mugs, and the rest of them clattered up the stairs. But when Diana was in her room and Beth was brushing her teeth, Elaine pulled Anthony down the hall and into her secret hiding place again.

They crawled in and pulled the boxes together behind them.

"Are you worried about Daddy coming tomorrow?"

"I suppose so."

Elaine sighed. "Believe me, we all are. But I want you to stay. Listen -- will you be my blood brother?"

"All right -- but no real blood. Miss Rice says that's dangerous."

"What, then? We have to seal it somehow."

"How about a solemn vow on the Bible?"

"Good! I know where one is, right there in the cupboard." Elaine crawled out and was soon back again with a large, old Bible with a heavy clasp on it.

"I, Elaine, swear you will be my brother always, so help me God."

"I, Anthony, swear you will be my sister always, so help me God."

"Now we have to shake hands three times."

"All right, sister." They smiled at each other.

"Do you think that's enough?"

"If we mean it, it is."

They were silent for a moment. Then, "You want to see where we're listed in the Bible?"

"All right."

Elaine turned on her pencil light and opened to the back of the Bible where, in bold black ink, the births, marriages and deaths of several generations had been entered.

One entry caught Anthony's eye immediately: Anthony Richard Martin Thornby. Signed with pride. The first-born son and heir of those grandparents that Sam had told them about. Anthony touched it with a finger.

"See? There's me. Elaine Antoinette Thornby."

"Antoinette? That's like me!"

"Yes, I was named after Uncle Tony. He had just died. See?"

"Yes." Anthony chewed on his finger, feeling jumpy and nervous. Just above Elaine's name was the bare record of that other Anthony's death, and Anthony could see the grief in the writing. Somehow Anthony knew, looking at it, that he should never have tried to come here. It was invading a family's private grief. And anyway, it was just a silly dream, as silly as all the other hopes at Washburn.

"Come on, we ought to go." Leaving Elaine to put the Bible away, Anthony stumbled to his feet and hurried to the privacy of his own room, his heart thumping painfully. He threw himself on the bed, still seeing that name in the Bible, as if it were burned into his brain.

And then the tears came.

C H A P T E R   15
****

Saturday morning dawned bright and cold. Anthony woke suddenly from a nightmare in which a horribly deformed man was reaching for him with thin, claw-like fingers. After the first moment of fright, he grinned ruefully to himself, recognizing both the horror movie he and Gerry and seen two weeks ago, and the anxiety he was feeling about meeting the earl.

He lay in bed for a moment, looking around the bare little room that already seemed dearly familiar and preciously private, and had to blink rapidly at the thought that in all probability, he would not be sleeping here again. How would it happen? The earl would come home, call the police, and they would take him away -- would it be like that?

He cringed, and pulled the blankets up over his head. To be hauled away like a common criminal -- no, surely SHE would not allow that.

But his heart sank. She had said she couldn't stand up to him.

Perhaps it would be more dignified to leave before the earl arrived. Go back to Three Chimneys,

today, and see what turned up.   But that would be
taking advantage of the Stoners -- they worked so
hard, what would they really want with an extra mouth
to feed?

Then -- go the police in York, himself, and get
sent back to the Home...?   It wasn't SO bad there.
And he would make more of an effort, this time, to
adjust to the Home, to try and make it more of a
family, as he had pledged with Elaine and Diana and
Beth.

Besides, if he didn't wait to tangle with the
earl, perhaps he could still stay friendly with them
-- go and visit them in London. Anthony brightened.
He could even take Gerry, sometimes. They could go to
the opera, perhaps go horse-back riding in the park --
perhaps he could even go with them to one of the
Queen's garden parties. He would dearly love to meet
the Queen. Well, why not? After all, it was an
earl's family; surely they got invited. Didn't they?

Anthony frowned. He wasn't sure of anything any
more. Perhaps they didn't.   This wasn't a family like
any earl's family he had ever imagined.

But yes, it was better to leave today. With a
heavy heart, he got up and started dressing. Look on
the bright side, he told himself fiercely: haven't I
had a whole week, almost, living in a castle with
a real countess, and real Ladies? I had no right to
expect so much.

It really had been a stupid idea, he admitted to
himself ruefully. Gerry had been right. It was far
better just to make friends with people, like Marc

Elliot or the Stoners at Three Chimneys, and perhaps something might come of that, and perhaps not, but it least it was a relationship based on honest friendship, not on a daydream.

He sat down on the bed to pull on his shoes, and then looked around the room again, feeling reluctant to go. He walked over to look out the window, up to the pine trees where they had gone to collect wood.

Well, it had been an adventure. A nice one, really. He sighed again, and straightened his back. He'd have breakfast, say his thank yous and goodbyes, and then go. They would understand.

But they didn't understand.

"Oh, Anthony, you can't go!" wailed Elaine. "We need you to explain about the castle's history, and be in the play, and everything!"

"We'll never be able to face Father if you're not here," Diana said with a worried look at her mother.

"Are you as much of a coward as the rest of us, after all?" Beth said, challenging him.

Anthony turned to their mother, and she held out her hand to him. "It'll be all right," she said a little uncertainly. "I wrote to him about you, so it can't be a surprise. And if he hasn't done anything about it yet, why worry? Please stay."

"You wrote to him, Mother?" Beth turned to her in surprise. "What did you say?"

"Just that Anthony had run away from that Home in London, and was staying with us -- heavens, Anthony, you never wrote, did you? I forgot!"

Anthony shook his head, and Elaine suppressed a grin.

The countess went on, "And that we were waiting for him to advise us about what to do."

"That sounds all right, then," Beth said hopefully. "If he already knows..."

"Why did you have to tell him anything?" Elaine said grumpily, but Beth's elbow prevented her from continuing.

She glowered at Beth, but Beth whispered, "It bought Anthony some time, didn't it? Don't be angry with Mother."

Elaine's frown melted away, and she turned to her mother eagerly. "But now we'll ask him if Anthony can stay with us always, can't we, Mother? We're blood brothers -- not with blood," she added hastily. "We took a solemn vow on the Bible."

The countess's face looked worried and uncertain. Her eyes shifted away from the girls' imploring looks. "Melby Place isn't ours, so we could hardly invite Anthony to stay with us there." She turned and looked anxiously at Anthony. "It's not that we don't want you," she added. "I'd like that. Really, I would."

"Then everything depends on whether we can persuade Daddy to let us live here again," Diana said eagerly. "We just HAVE to."

"We WILL persuade him," Elaine said fiercely. She linked her arm with Anthony's, and Beth took his other arm.

"Yes, we will," Beth said, and Diana glanced at her with some amusement. "But you've got to stay and face the music with the rest of us, Anthony, really you must, you can see that! We're all in this together, YOU said. You can't just run off when things get tough!"

"Yes, after all," Diana said with a smile, "here we are, ALL of us wanting to run away, from Melby Place at least -- and you're the only one who's managed it so far. You're our good example! You wouldn't be so cruel as to leave us to our fate alone, would you?"

"Yes, knight-errant, what do you say to that?" Beth pulled teasingly on Anthony's arm.

Everyone was smiling by now, and Anthony gave up. "All right, all right. But how about getting one last load of wood in, before the snows come, so Sam won't have to do it when he comes back?"

"Good idea. I'll come, too," the countess said. "Let's not sit around here all day, thinking."

"Heavens, no, not that." Diana put her arm around her mother. "It's going to be all right, anyway. We'll make it turn out all right."

If the others were not so sure, they tried not to show it, and except for a certain tightness in the stomach which made everyone feel not very hungry for lunch, the day went on in a flurry of activity. There was the wood to get, the portrait to finish, and then Beth, of all people, got the idea that the castle should be cleaned and dusted, swept and polished, in order to impress their father. Then Diana got inspired to provide a special tea -- so there was a lot to be done.

Then, all too soon, they heard the Morris chugging up the drive.

They all fell silent, and Anthony could feel the knot in his stomach grow tighter.

The door opened, and the earl limped in.

From their talk about the accident, Anthony had expected someone horribly mutilated, but actually, the long, thin scar down one side of the earl's face only made him look interesting. And the limp was barely noticeable.

He's not a monster after all, Anthony thought with relief. Like Richard the Third wasn't. Elaine had told him that the story about him being deformed was almost certainly an exaggeration.

The girls all met their father at the door with hugs, which seemed to surprise him. Anthony and Lady Daphne hung back. The earl greeted them all, and then noticed Anthony.

"Well, and who's this?" His voice didn't sound angry or upset.

"You remember, Roger; I wrote to you about Anthony." The countess put her arm protectively around Anthony's shoulders.

"Oh. I'm sorry. I mislaid that letter before I had a chance to read it." His hand crept unconsciously toward his pocket. "So you'll have to tell me again."

The girls glanced at each other in dismay.

"Anthony's a friend of mine, who's staying for tea," Elaine put in hurriedly.

The earl looked puzzled. "Is there a new family in the village?"

"Tea's ready," Diana sang out, and Elaine and Beth ran to the table in relief.

With that awkward moment over, they sat down at the table by the fire. The table had been carefully set with the best damask tablecloth and the good china, and red candles burned in the antique silver candlesticks.

"What a nice home-coming!" The earl looked startled and pleased.

He started serving up the chicken and gravy, while the girls kept up a nervous chatter about their visit to Sam, their gathering of the wood, and so on, in order to keep him from asking any more questions about Anthony.

"And mother has done a portrait of Anthony. It's super, Daddy! You will show it to him, too, won't you, Mother?"

Her mother looked down at her plate, hesitating.

"You've all seen it, have you?" The earl sounded a bit put out. "You aren't afraid of showing it to me, are you, Daphne?"

"Yes, she is," Beth was saying. "Maybe you shouldn't always be a critic, Daddy. Mother needs encouragement."

The countess's face was turning pink. "Have some salad, Roger," she said hurriedly.

Rothwick smiled a bit grimly.

"We've written a play, Daddy." Elaine looked at him hopefully. "It's great fun -- it's Diana's, really, but we made it longer. It's all about Rothwick -- the curse, and the secret room, and Richard the Third, and Bosworth and nobody coming back -- and we changed centuries a bit to make the young widow of Bosworth be your mother, so we could get in the part about the three rivals and the actress from London."

Rothwick snorted. "Who's been telling you that tale? Anyway, there weren't any actresses in Richard's day -- all the parts were played by men."

Elaine's face fell, but Beth forced a laugh. "That would be even funnier, then, wouldn't it? Have it be a male actor who unmasks himself after he's showed them up?"

"What a bizarre sense of humor you have," Rothwick murmured.

"It doesn't have to be an actress," Elaine suggested, her face brightening. "How about a court beauty?"

"Sounds interesting, at least," Rothwick said drily. "I take it I'm to see THAT, at least?"

The countess glanced at him in surprise.

"Yes, we'll perform it tonight, if you aren't too tired," Diana said eagerly. "The reason we wrote it..."

The countess broke in. "How about some trifle, everyone?" She glanced at Diana with a warning look, and Diane frowned impatiently. Couldn't they ask him and get it over with?

Elaine sighed and started clearing the table. The earl looked at her in amazement, and then turned to Diana. "I don't believe you've attempted trifle before."

"Oh, Mother made it," Diana said absently.

"Your mother!" The earl's astonishment increased. He shut his mouth firmly, as if not wanting to say the wrong thing.

The pink was rising in the countess's cheeks again.

"We've had such fun up here this time," Elaine said wistfully, as she and Anthony and Beth cleared the table.

"What's been going on here?" Rothwick asked his wife quizzically as the others all left for the kitchen.

"It has really been very nice indeed," she said cautiously. "It's been good to have someone else around, someone pleasant and helpful like Anthony. He's been good for us all. But tell me how things are going in London," she added hastily, backing off the subject of Anthony.

Rothwick sighed. "As detestably as ever..." He stopped as the girls came back with dessert.

"Well, Anthony, these girls have hardly given you a chance to say boo," Rothwick began. "Do you live..."

But all three girls broke in at once.

"Do you know the artist..."

"Did we tell you..."

"I'm learning to..."

Rothwick looked around with some amusement.
"Let's have it one at a time. Diana?"

"I--I'm learning to crochet -- mother and I are
making things for Christmas. It's fun..." She
stopped, trying frantically to think of more to say.
She wasn't use to making conversation with her father.
She glanced at Elaine with an appeal in her eyes.

"And I'm learning to cook! We baked some cakes
for Sam. But I wondered if you knew the artist,
Marcus Elliot, Daddy? Mother says he's well known."

"I've heard of him, of course. Has he been up
here?"

"Oh no, we haven't met him. Anthony met him..."
Too late, Elaine realized that she'd led the conversation back to Anthony. She bit her lip.

"Oh?" Rothwick looked over at Anthony, and Beth
broke in, sounding breathless.

"Did we tell you the joke about what note does a
piano play if it's dropped down a mine shaft?"

"I give up."

"A flat miner!" The girls laughed loudly.

"But what was all that about Marcus Elliot?"
Rothwick looked confused.

"Do you know the joke about the old empty barn?"

Rothwick frowned. "What is all this? I'm
beginning to smell something fishy!"

There was a stricken silence.

"Well? What's going on?"

The countess pushed her dish away. "Well, I did
write to you about it, Roger. It's Anthony. He's run
away from an orphan's home in London..."

She stopped, puzzled, as her husband's face went quite pale. He looked sharply at Anthony with disbelief and hostility, and then the blood rose in his face in an angry rush. His cup clattered into his saucer and he half stood, leaning on the table.

"Yes, it's been on the news. Anthony Richard Martin, they said." He spoke the name cuttingly, and the girls and their mother stared at him, and then at Anthony, shock in their faces. That was a name none of them were likely to forget.

Anthony felt the blood drain from his face. He stared at the earl, unable to face the others. What would they think of him now?

"So this is where you came," the earl went on sarcastically. "Expecting us to think you were one of the family, I take it! In fact, looking to take over as earl, no doubt, with some trumped-up lie about being my brother's child. Eh?" His eyes were ice cold, and his voice was enough to freeze the veins.

Anthony looked at him in bleak dismay, unable to speak.

"You don't bother to deny it, I see." Rothwick went on, his voice steel-hard, and rising in anger. "Do you realize what an insult that is to my brother, to me, to this whole family? You common little guttersnipe! Do you really suppose that my brother would leave his child to be brought up in an orphan home? In any case, it is quite impossible that my brother could have associated himself with the kind of common -- person -- your mother must have been..."

"You leave my mother out of this!" Anthony leaped to his feet, his eyes blazing with anger.

The two stared at each other for a heated moment. Then Anthony went on, his anger giving him courage, "You have no right to speak so about my mother. At least **common** people are kind to each other -- you wouldn't know about that, would you! Oh, what's the use! I meant to leave this morning -- I should have done it." He turned and ran to the door.

"Anthony..." Beth jumped up, knocking over her chair.

"Wait, Anthony!" Elaine threw her father a look of hatred, and ran after Anthony.

The earl's rage was in a state of suspension as he looked around at his remaining family. They all seemed to be looking at him accusingly.

"Daddy, how could you!"

Beth's cry started his rage boiling again. "That'll be all, young lady!"

Rothwick limped stiffly to the library door and disappeared behind it.

"That does it," the countess said slowly. She got up, squared her shoulders as if for battle and followed her husband to the library.

Diana and Beth looked at each other anxiously.

"What'll we do?" whispered Beth.

Diana sighed. "Might as well wash up." They looked at each other with sympathy. "We might have known."

The countess shut the library door behind her.

Rothwick was laying a fire in the fireplace and didn't
look up.

The countess took a deep breath. "The boy will
freeze to death out on the moors tonight. Haven't you
heard that snow is expected? He was our invited
guest, and we have a responsibility to go out and find
him and bring him back. Will you go, or shall I?"

Rothwick looked up at her in astonishment. This
wasn't the usual cool, detached Daphne. Furthermore,
there was some sense in what she was saying. He stood
up, brushing wood chips off his trousers as he thought
about it. He looked at her, hesitating, seeing how
lovely she looked, especially with her face looking
alive again, her eyes snapping and her cheeks pink.

Then he smiled at her, and it was her turn to
look astonished. Roger never smiled any more -- and
in the middle of one of his rages? She looked at him
uncertainly.

"I'll go and look for him, Daphne. You and the
girls hold the fort."

Daphne looked at him suspiciously. "What are you
playing at?"

"The boy is a cheat and a fraud -- I don't at all
like the way he seems to have wormed his way into your
good graces -- but I'll not have him dying on Rothwick
land."

"He's not like that, Roger. He's a nice boy."

"Nice boys don't go around trying to pretend they
belong in a family when they don't."

"He never said a word about that."

Rothwick made an unbelieving noise.

"I think it's time you paid some attention to what the rest of your family thinks, Roger."

"If you had ever bothered to tell me what you thought, of course I would have listened."

"I'm telling you now -- that boy is no fraud!"

"He didn't deny coming here because of that silly coincidence of names -- it's true he may actually have been named after Tony -- they often take names out of the newspapers at these places -- but that doesn't give him any right..."

"He probably simply wanted to find out if there was any connection. Wouldn't you have wanted to know, if you were he? He has a lot of pluck to come all the way up here on his own. Can't you give him credit for that, instead of seeing it as an insult? Anyway, he was telling the truth about wanting to leave this morning, before you got here. We all talked him out of it. I told him you knew about it, since I'd written to you. I didn't realize you never bothered to read my letters!"

"Daphne..."

"The boy simply wants a family, as any orphan would. I admire that. Although he certainly didn't pick out a very good one, did he!" Daphne turned her back.

Rothwick sighed. "I'll need to get started if I'm to find him." As he limped past her, she impulsively put her hand on his arm, and he paused in midstep.

"Do, really, find him, Roger. It's nearly dark already, and I'm worried about him."

"I'll find him. And when I come back, you and I need to have a talk."

She dropped her hand. "All right," she said uncertainly, peering at him.

He gave her a long look, and then, reluctantly, the earl went outside.

It had grown remarkably cold, even for the end of October, he thought. The sky was heavily overcast, and rapidly getting dark. He strained his eyes to look around the horizon, but saw nothing moving. He shouted twice, but the wind whipped the words away.

With a sigh of resignation, he got into his car. First the police constable, he decided. Then the road. Surely a city boy would head for the road, not across the moors. A pox on the boy!

CHAPTER 16
****

When Elaine had gone out, she had had to run to catch up with Anthony, who was in a state of quiet rage and despair. With much coaxing, she had persuaded him that there was no point in freezing to death out on the moors.

Eventually, she got him to promise to spend the night in her secret hiding place.

"You're already shivering now," she said anxiously, "and it's getting colder by the minute."

"It's just because I'm angry."

"Just the same!"

"All right -- but I'm off at first light!"

"Oh, Anthony, where will you go?" Elaine brushed the tears out of her eyes.

"Don't cry. Maybe I'll go back to Three Chimneys, at Selby. I might be able to stay there. If not --" he shrugged. "-- I'll go to the police and they'll ship me back to London. It's all right, honestly."

"You won't forget you're my brother?"

"Of course not." Anthony's rage was evaporating. "Come on, now. I've promised to stay inside tonight, haven't I? Much against my wishes. Now you have to get me there without being seen, and say goodbye, and go back before YOU freeze to death -- and don't forget to pretend you couldn't find me!"

Elaine led him around through the kitchen and up the back staircase to the secret hide-out. She gave him her pencil light, and then, almost hurriedly, left to go downstairs. Neither of them said goodbye.

Anthony lay uncomfortably in the hide-out, wishing he had not promised to stay, feeling miserable and alone, in spite of his brave words to Elaine, and alternately feeling outcaste, angry, and ashamed.

Had SHE turned against him, too, after what her husband had said? Oh, he would never try such a stupid thing again -- it was too painful all around. With a feeling of homesickness, he thought of Washburn, and let the tears fall.

Anthony awoke from a fitful sleep, and for a moment was puzzled as to where he was. He was still half in a dream he'd been having, in which he was back at Three Chimneys. Pops was guiding his hand over the mason's mark in the fireplace, and chanting, "He was a builder, builder, builder, fell off the roof, the roof, the roof."

Slowly, Anthony became more aware of where he was, and why, and sighed unhappily. He was a builder, builder -- a builder of secret rooms!

Anthony felt his scalp start to tingle as the thought occurred to him. And he fell off the roof -- or was he thrown?

Wide awake now, Anthony sat up and pushed cautiously at the boxes that enclosed him. All was dark, all was quiet. There was one way to tell whether Rothwick had been built by Robert Stoner of Three Chimneys -- the fireplace in the kitchen.

Putting Elaine's pencil light in his pocket and carrying his shoes in his hand, Anthony crept silently from the room, along the cold passageway, and down the staircase. His heart beating faster, he opened the door to the kitchen and closed it slowly, silently, after him. The moon shone in at the window, and he padded swiftly to the wide fireplace. His feet were freezing, so he stopped to put on his shoes, almost afraid to look for the Jerusalem cross of Robert Stoner.

Then he shone the light up under the left-hand side of the mantelpiece, where the mark had been at Three Chimneys. The stones were black with soot, and the light was not very bright. Anthony picked up a knife and brushed at the soot, looking for an indentation.

There -- was that it? Using more pressure, he scraped away at the soot, as gradually the outline of a mark emerged. The Jerusalem cross! A shiver shook Anthony as he thought of Robert Stoner, 500 years ago and more, making that mark to sign his work. And only he, Anthony, had known where to look -- and what it would mean -- he knew where the secret room might be!

Shaking with eagerness, Anthony shone the torch along the wall. Yes, the layout was very like that at Three Chimneys. Why hadn't he noticed it before? There was where the door had been knocked through. And yes, just there was a large square cupboard in the wall, just like Pops had said, the cupboard where Diana kept the laundry basket. Anthony moved it to the floor.

Now then, what had Pops said? Anthony racked his brain. A way to unlock it, and then push at the back of the cupboard. But how to unlock it?

THINK, Anthony told himself, forcing himself to stand quietly. Way of the cross -- the Rothwicks had supposed that meant the chapel. They had probably never thought to look in the kitchen. But knowing the story about the wine barrels being called the "way of the cross" made it just as sensible that a place where wine was kept could be the right place. Might Robert Stoner have told that story to the earl? And this cupboard looked as if it could have originally been intended for a wine barrel.

Then "tears of tross, Norman dross." Norman could mean a reference to French, as the Rothwicks had already figured out. Trousse? Oh boy, my French isn't up to much, Anthony thought. But if "cross" was "croix," how about trois, three? Tears of -- that could be "tirez!" Pull the third?

Excited, Anthony played the light around the cupboard opening, and stopped it directly above, where four stone hooks protruded, a sort of decoration that he had never noticed.

Pull the third! Anthony quietly lifted a chair to the wall, climbed up, and pulled on the third hook.

Nothing happened.

Remembering that no one had used it for at least 400 years, Anthony put his foot against the wall and used all his strength.

With a sudden click, the hook pulled out about two inches, nearly throwing Anthony off balance. It worked!

One more thing: Norman dross. If tross was trois, then dross might be -- droit! To the right? Again Anthony put his strength into pulling the stone to the right, and was rewarded with another click as the stone moved sluggishly into place.

Biting his lip in excitement, his heart pounding, Anthony climbed into the cupboard and pushed at the back. It gave way suddenly, propelling Anthony forward into a black hole, where he struck his head hard against the cupboard door before it slipped back into place.

Anthony, knocked unconscious, fell to the floor.

Anthony woke up with a headache, and lay for a moment, rubbing his forehead, before realizing that he was also cold, and uncomfortable. He frowned. Where was he? He opened an eye cautiously, but everything was dark. He sat up, holding his head. Then he remembered: he was in the secret room!

He felt around him for the pencil light, found it, and flicked it on. He was on the stone floor of a small room similar to Pop's room at Three Chimneys.

The secret door had shut itself, and Anthony hastened to try it, to make sure he wasn't locked in. But it opened easily from inside. It could be locked and unlocked from inside, as well as from the kitchen.

Thank goodness for that! He didn't relish joining whatever "workmen's bones" might be lying about.

Eyes wide, but eager to explore, he shut the door again and flashed the light about him.

There was a small oak chest and two stools. Tapestries hung on the walls, and in the corner, as at Three Chimneys, a winding stone staircase led upwards.

A little stiffly, from lying on the cold floor, Anthony climbed the stairs. The room above had panelled walls, pale wood from floor to ceiling, like the library. The ceiling was arched and carved, and the floor was covered with carpets. Compared with the room below, this was quite cozy!

Walking cautiously across the carpets, which raised dust at every step, Anthony crossed to a carved oak table and chairs, and a writing desk, which were the only pieces of furniture.

Beyond the desk, a narrow passage led to still another room, similar to the last, but furnished this time with a large bed, hung with disintegrating curtains. The whole thing looked as if it would fall apart at a touch. A fireplace was carved out of the inner wall.

Feeling a bit dizzy with his discoveries, as well as from the blow on his head, Anthony let himself gingerly onto the bed, raising a cloud of dust that made him sneeze. At least it was better than the floor, he thought drowsily.

When he awoke, feeling better, he began to realize how much this would mean to Elaine and her family. At least I can give them something now, and leave with some pride, he thought with a lift of spirits. Instead of -- getting kicked out. But I'd better finish exploring first.

There was some daylight coming in from a further passageway, which led out to the south wall. Following it, he found a tiny window, hidden from outside view by the great coat of arms over the main door. He could look down at the car park through a tiny slit, and was surprised to see snow on the ground. So the Rob had been right! It really must have been cold last night. Thank goodness Elaine had persuaded him to come inside!

In the passage, another dim light showed, and Anthony found it was a tiny peep hole, hidden among the decorations near the ceiling of the great hall, through which he could see most of the room. There was a wooden cover which could be used to hide the peep-hole from inside.

But suddenly he realized that the Rothwicks' car had not been down in the car park, and tire tracks had crossed the snow. The angle of daylight meant, in fact, that it was past noon already. The Rothwicks must have left. His heart sank. They had returned to London, then, and had left Anthony, not caring what had happened to him.

But he mustn't think of that. The main thing was, he was still on his own. In fact, could he be locked in?

For a moment he held his breath, but then, remembering that Sam's daughter would be up in a few days and that there was a supply of tins in the kitchen, he brightened. It might be fun to be king of the castle for a few days!

He went back to the bedroom, and noticed something under the bed. He must have dislodged it when he lay down.

He reached down for it and straightened up. It was a piece of parchment, and it was hard to make out what it said. He took it to the peephole for more light, and struggled to make out the strange letters.

By the third reading, he began to realize what it might be, and shook with excitement.

But just then he heard a noise below. The Rothwicks back? His heart gave a leap. He looked down into the hall.

Expecting, and dreading, to see the Rothwicks, it took several seconds for the sight to sink in. It wasn't the Rothwicks, it was those three men from the lorry!

"See? Piece of cake. And they'll be looking for a man with a mustache." The man in the sheepskin jacket peeled the hair off his lip and put it in his pocket.

"All right, no time to lose," he went on briskly. "I'll go through the house and put a red tag on everything we want. We'll gather it all here by the door for wrapping, and then it will be easier to see how to load it all in. We'll start with the library."

With increasing apprehension, Anthony saw one of the men lean a rifle against the wall by the door. The three men moved into the library, and Anthony stared down in horror, his mouth dry.

They were stealing the castle's one asset, the antique furniture! How could he stop them?

C H A P T E R 17
****

It was dark, and the roads and fields were covered with a light layer of snow, before Rothwick got back to the constable's cottage. The other four searchers turned up right behind him. They had all been checking different areas.

"Any luck?" Rothwick called out as he emerged from the Morris.

"Nobody up towards Broxa."

"This snow cover makes it easier to spot footprints, and there certainly weren't any in the dale."

"He must have found some shed to crawl into for the night."

"Either that, or some motorist picked him up and he's in York by now."

The constable grunted. "Thank you for helping with the search, Will, Jim, Pete. But we'll not find him tonight. You may as well go home. We'll try again come morning."

"I can't pretend I'm not worried about the boy, though." John Bradford, the police constable, spoke in a low voice to Rothwick as the others left. "How did he happen to go out in this weather?"

Rothwick sighed. He and John had played together as boys, and John had always seen right through him. It must make him a good policeman if everyone felt, as he did, that they might as well tell him the truth. "It's all my fault. Afraid I was a bit hard on the boy. He ran out -- and there's been no sign of him since."

"Rob met him in the village with your daughters the other day."

"Ah, Rob." Rothwick looked at the steady gray eyes and sighed. "I was hard on him, too, wasn't I, some years back. I owe him an apology. I expect I owe a lot of people an apology."

"We'd all be happy for you if you could find more contentment in your life," John said quietly.

Rothwick took a deep breath, and his mouth twisted again. "That's very generous of you."

He glanced at John, wondering if that had sounded patronizing. But John was gazing at him with sober friendliness.

"Your girls seem happier now, at least. This is the first time in years that anyone in the village has seen them going about together."

Rothwick peered at him, startled. I suppose that's true, he thought. He felt a pang of regret. Had they all been as lonely as he was? He glanced at John again, envying him his air of being at peace with himself and the world.

"About the boy," John was saying. "The tracking hound from York is coming at first light. You'll let me know if he turns up at the castle? The boy, I mean, not the hound." They laughed companionably.

"I will," Rothwick promised, and got back into his car. Then he looked thoughtfully at the other man.

"It's been nice to see a little of you this time, even if it is on this wretched business. I'm afraid I haven't been very sociable when we've been up -- anxious to have a little peace and quiet after London, I suppose... We ought to go fishing together, come spring."

John nodded. "You should move back. This is the place for you."

Rothwick groaned. "Wish I could!"

The other man looked at him quietly in the dark. Then he sighed and stepped back. "Stop by before you leave tomorrow. If I'm out searching, Margaret can tell you if there's been any news."

"I'll do that. Thanks, John."

John nodded, and Rothwick drove off.

By the time he returned, the girls had been sent to bed, and Daphne was waiting for him.

"Oh, Roger, you -- you didn't find him!"

"Not a trace. I'm sorry."

Daphne bit her lip. "Well -- he's really very sensible. I almost trust him to be all right -- except for this snow -- oh, I wish you had found him!"

"Daddy?" The three girls, in dressing gowns, peered in at the door.

"I'm sorry, girls, he has undoubtedly holed up somewhere safe. There was no sign of him."

"Then you're not still angry with him?" Elaine sounded relieved.

Rothwick hesitated. "I'd really rather not hear any more about him just now. He's caused enough trouble."

Four faces fell, and the earl began to feel irritated again.

"Daddy --" Diana hesitated. "We'd like to talk to you about something else. We'd like to move back to Rothwick. We've talked about it -- a lot -- how we could make the castle pay this time -- we're all older now, so we won't have to hire anyone to help, and we don't need any more brochures, and if we start in time we can get free advertising..."

"It won't work." The earl's frustration was growing.

"Roger, you said you'd listen! We're trying to tell you that we're very unhappy in London, and we'd like to work out with you how we could come back here. Perhaps you could find something to do in York that you could really enjoy. And I'd be glad to work, too..."

The earl, pale, spoke quietly. "Thank you, that's all I'd need in order to feel a total failure, to have my wife go out and work, not to be able to send my children to a decent school. No! Now go to bed, all of you! We're leaving in the morning, and I don't want to hear another word!"

"Daddy..."

"No!"

"Roger..."

"No!" The beleaguered earl made his escape to bed, himself, and the rest trooped disconsolately behind.

Breakfast was a silent affair the next morning, with everyone looking tired, including the earl. Even the snow on the ground aroused no enthusiasm. The earl was beginning to feel very much out-numbered.

He felt even more so when he found everyone else going to the kitchen for the washing up. He tried to promote the idea of leaving for London early, and met stiff resistance.

"We **can't** go until Anthony is found, Roger," his wife said firmly.

"The police constable was going to get in touch with his headquarters this morning if he hadn't turned up." Roger struggled to keep his voice neutral. That dratted boy! "We can't do any more here, and in fact with no phone here we'd be LESS likely to be kept informed. And since he'll be returned to London in any case..."

"Oh Daddy, this is all WRONG," Diana burst out, taking courage from her mother. "We belong HERE, and -- and so does Anthony..."

"I already have a family, and they're more than enough to cope with." Rothwick spoke more sharply.

"And suppose he IS Tony's son?"

Rothwick glared at his wife, angry words rushing to his lips.

But he couldn't say them. What if he were Tony's child? No! It wasn't possible. But IF... No! His mind in a turmoil, he frowned fiercely. "He hasn't got the slightest family resemblance."

"Neither have I!" His wife's jaw was set stubbornly.

They stared angrily at each other for a long moment. At last Rothwick threw up his arms in frustration. "I can't cope with staying here while all of you give me such black looks. I want you all in the car in five minutes, and that's final!

Beth smiled grimly. "Speaking of a family resemblance, any resemblance we have to a family is purely coincidental."

Rothwick banged his tea cup down on the saucer, and Beth left hurriedly.

Diana and Elaine followed more slowly.

The trainer arrived at the door with the tracking hound, asking for something Anthony had handled. Rothwick gave him the pillow he had been using, and Daphne bit her lip, looking worried.

Nearly an hour later, after several delaying tactics, the car started off. They stopped in the village, but there was no news of Anthony.

They went on in moody silence for another several miles. As they neared York, Elaine began to sing "Ilka Moor," defiantly, and everyone except Rothwick joined in. Pride and surprise kept him from singing with them.

Beth's wrong, he thought with wonder. They HAVE become a family again. Without me. It jolted him into realizing how separate they had been before.

Could that blasted boy really have had something to do with this change in them?

Daphne spoke quietly from beside him. "I can't live in London much longer, Roger."

"I'm trapped there. You know that."

"Are you? Or are you still punishing yourself for the accident?"

He stiffened. "If I am, isn't that my affair?"

"Not if we're all punished with you. Do we deserve that?"

Rothwick was silent.

Suddenly Elaine's head was thrust between them. "Stop, oh stop! Diana says it snowed LAST NIGHT!"

"What on earth are you going on about?" Rothwick asked crossly.

"Oh Daddy, I -- I made Anthony sleep in the castle last night. He didn't want to -- I promised not to tell -- he was going to leave at first light. I checked this morning and he wasn't there, but -- don't you see? I thought it had snowed this morning, after he'd gotten away. But if it snowed last night, and there were no footprints..."

The car slowed to a stop. Rothwick turned to face Elaine, his scar a dangerous color. "Young lady, do you realize that you've caused several men to go out in the snow for half the night, looking for a boy who wasn't missing?"

Elaine sank back in her seat, silenced for once.

Beth gave her a sympathetic look. "But Daddy,

the point is, he may be locked up in the castle. We'll have to go back."

There was a dead silence -- not even a sound of breathing.

"I give up."

Four faces lit up. "Oh, great..."

"Not so fast. I'M going back -- but I'll put you on the train in York so that you won't be up half the night and miss school tomorrow -- and so you won't be able to interfere any further!"

"Oh Daddy!"

"That's enough wailing and moaning. Now be quiet!" Grimly, he started the car moving again.

There was a train just due, and Rothwick saw them all safely, if glumly, on board before turning his car northeast again. What a bother all this was. Not to mention the expense!

Preoccupied with his own thoughts, he had arrived at the castle and pulled up in front of the door before noticing the lorry parked along the wall.

"Hallo, what's this?" he thought as he got out. With a puzzled frown, he went in the open door and entered the great hall.

There in front of him were antiques from all over the castle, gathered together, wrapped with padding but still recognizeable to someone who treasured them so. Rothwick stopped, puzzled.

Two men were just wrapping the Lady Davenport desk from his wife's room, one of his favorite pieces.

"What the..."

And then it sank in.

Aghast, he stared at the two men, and they stared belligerently back. Rothwick felt his heart sink. It was all too obvious that the castle was being robbed. What could he do about it? And was that boy involved in this, too?

"The Earl of Rothwick, I think?" drawled a voice from behind him, and he turned to see a man with a rifle.

Rothwick said nothing, and the man laughed. "Oh, yes, you fit the description. What a pity you decided to return to the old family castle." He stepped aside from the door and motioned with the rifle. "Let's step into the kitchen. You two carry on."

Rothwick felt a chill. I've seen them, he thought. I doubt if they'll want to leave any witnesses. He tried to estimate how far he would have to leap in order to grab the rifle, but the man laughed again.

"Don't try it, mate," he said.

But Rothwick, desperate, did try, only to receive a blow from behind that sent him collapsing to the floor.

"Tie his hands behind his back and get him into the kitchen," he heard as if from a distance.

"Why not shoot him here?"

"Not on these expensive carpets, you dolt! Do as you're told!"

Rothwick felt his hands being pulled roughly to his back and tied. Then he was dragged into the kitchen and dropped onto the floor again.

"Now?"

"Now."

With horror, Rothwick twisted around in time to look directly into the barrel of the rifle, as the man squeezed the trigger.

C H A P T E R   18
****

There was a click, and all three of them looked at the rifle in amazement. Rothwick let his head fall back to the floor. He felt sick.

"You mean this thing wasn't loaded?" the leader asked angrily.

"I could have sworn..."

"There's more ammo out in the lorry. Come on, dunderhead, I'll show you." He gave a quick twist of the rope, tying Rothwick's arm to the heavy table leg.

They left, and Rothwick shut his eyes, feeling empty. They would soon be back, and it would all be over.

But suddenly there was another surprise as someone started sawing through the ropes with a kitchen knife. He opened his eyes to see Anthony. What the...

Anthony was pulling desperately at his arm. "In here, quick. Quick!"

Rothwick forced himself to his feet, and followed the boy into the cupboard and through the door at the

back. Anthony shut the door and shot home the lock,
and then blew his breath out.

"Whew, that was a close one!"

Rothwick looked around him in amazement, his
pulse quickening.

"Good lord, you've found it!" he blurted out.

"Sh! We'd better whisper. I don't know whether
they can hear us or not. Yes, I found it." Anthony
told him swiftly how he had worked it out.

"Then those men turned up," he went on, "so while
they were upstairs I whipped out to unload the rifle,
and then let the air out of one of their tyres, and
got the flare gun and brought it in here, but -- it
won't fit out the windows -- they're too small!"

Rothwick looked at him with respect, and then
blushed to think that the boy apparently bore him no
ill-will for what he had said. "Well, let's think,
then. What can we do?"

"If they have more ammunition in the lorry, as I
heard them say, then it's a bit more risky to be
moving about. And now that you've gone missing,
they'll be keeping more of an eye out. So perhaps we
don't have a very good chance of getting down to the
village. Oh, by the way, I took the lorry keys,
too..." Anthony pulled them from his pocket and
grinned.

"You've been busy!"

"But come on, we can hear what they're doing in
the great hall." Anthony led the way upstairs, and
noticed with pleasure Rothwick's amazed delight in the
two upper rooms. Then they were at the peep-hole.

"I tell you, I tied him good! Don't ask me how he got hold of a knife -- I'm surprised he could even stand up!"

"Well, get out there and fix the bloomin' tyre! And leave the rifle with me. I'll stand by where I can see both exits."

"Won't he be away from here by now? We ought to get out of here before he comes back with the police!"

"Use your head! There's snow on the ground. Do you see any footprints, except ours back and forth to the lorry?"

"N-no..."

"Well then! We've got him holed up somewhere in here. It's only a matter of time. We speed up the job and get out of here -- and leave some petrol splashed about -- won't it be a cryin' shame, poor old Rothwick Castle, burned to the ground -- with the poor old earl inside!"

Rothwick and Anthony looked at each other anxiously.

"Now get cracking with that tyre," the man went on. "Ben! Start bringing those smaller pieces out here for loading."

Anthony stepped back, biting his lip and frowning. "We'd better think of something, fast!"

Rothwick nodded, then winced and held his head.

Anthony looked around in desperation. He'd have to try making a run for it. Perhaps out a window at the back?

Then he snapped his fingers softly. "Got it!"

He beckoned Rothwick back into the bedroom, where he leaned into the fireplace and craned his neck upwards.

"There's a bit of a curve there, but then the chances are the chimney goes straight up, right?"

"Yes, I suppose, but what...?"

"Then I can fire the flare gun right up the chimney!"

"Anthony, you're a genius!"

Anthony was already tucking the flare gun into his belt and removing his jacket.

"You can walk yourself up it," Rothwick suggested as Anthony peered up, hesitating. "With your back against one wall and your feet against the other. I'll give you a start."

"Good. Here goes!"

Rothwick lifted him up into the chimney as far as he could, and Anthony began pushing himself up past the curve. In a moment Rothwick heard the whoosh of the flare gun going off. Then a rather black Anthony reappeared.

"Listen!" They crept back to the outside window, where they took turns looking down at the three men pointing to the flare and running about.

"What do you mean, you've lost the keys!" came a wail from below.

"Well, what about the car, then?" They lost a few more moments trying to start the Morris without a key, as Rothwick removed the keys from his own pocket and showed them to Anthony with a grin. "London habit," he whispered.

Then one of the men started running for the forest.

"Wait for me!" And the other two were running, too.

Rothwick clapped Anthony on the back, raising a cloud of soot. "We've done it! Or rather, YOU've done it! How can I thank you! But come on, we'd better go and warn the constable that they're armed."

They ran down the dim stairs, unlocked the secret door, and were out in the kitchen again.

"I don't understand how they got in," Rothwick panted as they ran out the front door. "I thought at first that perhaps..."

"That I'd let them in?" Anthony looked so shocked that Rothwick was sorry he'd mentioned it.

"I'm sorry - you can see how it looked..." They climbed into the Morris, and Rothwick started it up.

"The funny thing is, I rode up from London in the back of that lorry," Anthony confessed. "They didn't know I was there. But of course when they mentioned getting a key from a 'simple village maiden,' I didn't know they were talking about HERE!"

Rothwick frowned in astonishment. "You don't mean that Rose was in on this?"

"Oh no, they were going to give her some story."

"But how could they have known about her in the first place?" Rothwick's puzzled frown deepened. "What else did they say?"

Anthony frowned in thought, trying to remember. "They were talking about a couple of people: Arabella and -- Rydale, I think, that they were working for."

"Could it have been Rundale?"

"Yes, that's it."

"Good lord! We're supposed to be signing an agreement with them tomorrow, that would have put us right into their crooked pockets! Thank goodness we found out in time!" Rothwick took his eyes off the drive long enough to glance at Anthony. "You're quite some good-luck talisman for this family!"

Anthony wriggled with pleasure, as Rothwick grew silent, thinking. With information as valuable as this to give Frank, information that would save him thousands of pounds, as well as his reputation, I could finally get free! Rothwick pounded the steering wheel, and Anthony looked at him, startled.

Rothwick smiled. "You don't know how much you've helped me, Anthony. Maybe we CAN move back to Rothwick, after all. But there's the constable."

The Morris slewed to a stop, and the constable came alongside in his car. Rothwick rapidly outlined what had happened, and Bradford decided to go back and phone for reinforcements. "They won't get far, I can promise you," he shouted as he turned his car.

"Oh, and report that the runaway boy is found, and safe, will you? We'll get in touch later," Rothwick called out.

Bradford laughed. "So I gathered." He sped off.

Rothwick started up the car again, and they drove down to the telephone kiosk, where Rothwick dialed the number at Melby Place.

Anthony could hear him telling the story, and then there was a pause. "By the way, Frank, I'm resigning, as of right now. We'll be down to pick up our things, but we're moving back to Rothwick."

There was another pause; Rothwick held the phone away from his ear with a grimace, and then grinned at Anthony.

"Sorry, Frank, but that's it."

He put the phone down and walked out, looking younger and happier.

"Well, now, Anthony." Rothwick got in and put his arm around Anthony's shoulders. "I suppose we'd better go back and get you cleaned up."

"Yes sir. Oh, and there's something else I have to show you."

"Something else! What more are you going to pull out of your hat?"

"Richard's thorn."

"What?

"Anthony laughed gleefully. "You'll see."

Rothwick dumped Anthony into a bathtub for a scrub while he took his clothes outside for a brush.

Clean again, Anthony showed him how to open the secret door, and they went in once again to the secret rooms.

In the desk upstairs, where Anthony had droppped it, was the piece of parchment he had found.

"Let's take it to the kitchen, where there's more light," Anthony suggested. "It's hard to read."

When they were back at the kitchen table, Rothwick began haltingly to read, stumbling over the old script, but with an increasing note of excitement in his voice.

"To my dear uncle and rightful king, to whom I do swear my firm fealty, greetings. Sire, I acknowledge you as my king, and even more than that I reaffirm the love I have always borne you. There are things I must tell you, vital to us all. I beg you to believe me, and to be on your guard.

"When our mother sent us hither to Rothwick Castle, she believed it to be best for us. I pray you not to blame her. In truth, dear Uncle, my brother Edward is still a little mad, and calls himself king, so perhaps it was wise for us to be hidden from the world. It seems that the Edwards in our family are forceful and fiery in their temperament, while we Richards are practical and realistic. It is because we are alike, my uncle, that I trust you and do not believe the stories we have been told.

"But now I have overheard a rumor which distresses me, and it concerns you, my liege lord. I pray you..."

Rothwick set the parchment down almost reverently, and then looked at Anthony.

"That's all. Good lord. Richard's nephews. Richard's thorn! You were right!"

Anthony nodded. "That's what I guessed, too. I was thinking -- if their mother was afraid for them, especially if she thought young Edward was likely to get himself into trouble, it would make sense for her to hide them somewhere -- and if she didn't dare tell Richard, he would have a hard time saying he didn't know where they were, so maybe he just kept quiet, hoping Elizabeth Woodville would bring them back before it got too embarrassing."

"I don't suppose we'll ever really know, but that makes good sense to me. But won't the historians go mad when they get their hands on this! Good lord, Anthony, you've really brought good fortune to Rothwick, in so many ways! I should think tourists WOULD come here, now." He looked back at the letter. "Poor lads, sounds as if they were hurried out of here suddenly. More treachery, perhaps. I hope it wasn't a Rothwick!"

"Let's let the experts work it out," Anthony suggested. "The more they argue over it, the more publicity you'll get."

Rothwick looked at Anthony again, hardly knowing whether to laugh or cry. He felt an unfamiliar tightness in his throat.

"Anthony, I owe you a big apology, and a great many thanks. Will you forgive me for the things I said?"

Anthony, blushing, nodded his head. "If you'll forgive me!"

Rothwick put his hand on the table, palm upward, and Anthony shyly placed his own small one in it. They shook hands solemnly.

"My wife seems to think we need you here, and I must say I think she may be right, for once..."

Just then there was another commotion, as the rest of the family burst through the door.

"Roger," the countess said firmly, so intent on what she intended to say that she didn't even notice

Anthony. "We got off at Doncaster and came back. We're not going to London again, unless it's to pack up and move out. We've had enough, and we've come up with an ultimatum: I don't care whether Anthony is our nephew or not, we want him to live with us. We can't have him at Melby Place, where we don't want to be anyway, so we're going to live HERE! Whether you want to join us or not is up to you..." She stopped, astonished, as Rothwick started to laugh.

"You're too late, my dear Daphne! I've quit my job, and Anthony, I hope..." he turned to him with a question in his eyes, "...will join us in our family enterprise right here at Rothwick."

Anthony's face, looking as if the sun had just broken through the clouds, was enough answer.

The countess burst into tears, and Rothwick put his arms around her. "We'll start over, shall we?" he murmured, and she nodded, leaning her head against his shoulder.

The girls got over their shock and swooped to hug Anthony, shrieking with joy.

The countess wiped her eyes. "Let's have a cup of tea," she said happily. "Then I want everyone to come up to the castle's secret room -- my studio -- and see the painting I've started of my four children."

"Wait 'til we tell you..." Rothwick and Anthony both spoke at once, then looked at each other and laughed.

And they all laughed together, a family at last.

DIFFERENCES IN BRITISH AND AMERICAN WORDS

Chips: French fries
Cluedo: Clue (a detective game)
Conkers: horsechestnuts
Crisps: potato chips
Football: soccer
Kerb: curb
M-One: Motorway-One (a superhighway)
Nick: steal
Petrol: gasoline
Pong: smell, odor
Tea: not always just a cup of;
    sometimes a whole afternoon
    or evening meal
Toff: a "gentleman"
Tyre: tire